TO SAVE MR. SPOCK...

"If we don't have that strobolin in twenty hours, he'll die," McCoy stated flatly. "That's a minimal figure, but it's pretty accurate.

"I wouldn't like to have to stretch it even five minutes."

There was nothing more McCoy could say . . . just as there was nothing more he could do.

Probably there was nothing as agonizing to a doctor of McCoy's ability as knowing exactly what to do to cure a patient and simply not having the material to do it with!

STAR TREK
LOG FIVE

Alan Dean Foster

Based on the Popular Animated Series Created
by Gene Roddenberry

BALLANTINE BOOKS • NEW YORK

SBN 345-24532-6-125

First Printing: August, 1975

Cover art supplied by Filmation Associates

Printed in the United States of America

BALLANTINE BOOKS
A Division of Random House, Inc.
201 East 50th Street, New York, N.Y. 10022
Simultaneously published by
Ballantine Books, Ltd., Toronto, Canada

For my best friend, Fred Foldvary....
Who knew and had confidence years
before it all started....

CONTENTS

STAR TREK LOG FIVE

Log of the Starship *Enterprise*

Stardates 5527.0—5527.4 Inclusive

James T. Kirk, Capt., USSC, FC, ret.

Commanding

transcribed by
Alan Dean Foster

At the Galactic Historical Archives
on S. Monicus I
stardated 6111.3

For the Curator: JLR

PART I

THE
AMBERGRIS
ELEMENT

(Adapted from a script by Margaret Armen)

I

(Sun to Queen four plus two)

"Starrfleet Academy?" M'mar murmured wonderingly. "You werre trrained as a historrian, daughterr. Historry, sociology, anthrropology ... those werre yourr forrtes in school. Not physics or spatial engineerring or some such."

M'ress' mother reclined on the lounge, her expression one of concern, feline pupils of carved jet narrowed against the warm evening day of mid-summerset on Cait.

"Is it something else that's led you to this line of thinking, daughterr? Perrhaps something else trroubles you ... that boy, now ..."

M'ress made a soft sigh of exasperation. "It has nothing to do with N'nance, materr. Orr with V'rrone, orr D'irraj, orr any of my frriends. I've simply decided that ..."

"You've *decided*," M'mar whispered half to herself.

"... I want to learrn morre about people as they arre now instead of how they've been. Is that so surrprrising? Becoming a Federration Starrfleet officerr is the best way to do that."

"And what about yourr litterr mates? What do they think of this sudden switch in mid-stalk?"

M'ress looked smug. "Sister M'nass thinks I'm as crrazy as you do, but both brrotherr M'rest and M'sitt say it's wonderful ... and typically me."

"They'rre half rright," M'mar muttered. "Take carre, M'ress. As eldest of the litterr, you have a rresponsibility to set good examples forr them. Considerr that whateverr you do is likely to be copied."

"I rrealize that, materr," M'ress replied, tail flicking nervously from side to side. It was that very thought

3

which had caused her to delay the announcement this long. "But I'm deterrmined on this thing."

M'mar eyed her daughter appraisingly, but M'ress refused to break the stare. "All rright then," she finally conceded, "if you'rre bound on it, trry yourr best. By the Prrey, yourr academic evaluations are high enough. But bewarre, daughter, you could end up on a satellite-to-planet shuttle in some farr corrnerr of the galaxy and see no morre in a lifetime than that one cornerr."

"I'm not worrried about that, materr," M'ress countered, with the confidence of the young. "One thing at a time. Firrst I have to get into the Academy."

"And if you can't, despite yourr evaluations?"

"Then I'll apply forr trraining as common crrew, of courrse," she said matter-of-factly.

M'mar offerred the ultimate Caitian argument. "This will separrate the family."

Now M'ress was forced to look away, and her voice dropped. "I know, materr, but this is something I have in my hearrt and mind to trry. Paterr will underrstand."

"Yourr crrazy sirre underrstands everrything!" M'mar half spat. "You inherrited yourr foolishness from him! He even pretends to underrstand yourr poetrry." She quieted abruptly, held out a paw to stroke her daughter's forehead with. "Naturrally, we'll both brreak ourr dewclaws to help you make it. . . ."

(Satellite four to Probe six less one)

"The branch classifications have been posted!"

Lena, the human cadet-aspirant with whom M'ress was quartered at the Academy, burst into the room. Her face was flushed, her breath racing.

Instantly the hair on M'ress' neck rose. Her tail flicked from side to side, bottled up. Lena caught her breath long enough to answer her roommate's unasked question.

"We both made the twenty percent cut. That's all I know, Kit."

M'ress relaxed to the point of collapse. Only the top

fifth of all applicants who were accepted to Starfleet were passed on for the full multi-year course of training. Now the arduous six-month ordeal of endless tests—physical as well as mental—was over ... and she had made it, she had actually made it!

Almost as one they reached for the switch which would activate the tiny computer screen each room came equipped with. Lena hit it first. The rectangle lit, and the words AWAITING INPUT appeared. At that point the enormity of their accomplishment supplanted the initial excitement, and the fear that it was all a dream took over.

"You do it, Lena ... you firrst."

"No ... I can't. All of a sudden, I can't."

"I'll rriddle you forr it."

"Oh no!" Lena grinned warily. "You're much too good at word games for me." She let her gaze travel around the immaculately kept room, eventually spotted the ancient toy top resting on the pile of workbooks.

"I'll spin you a dredel for it."

"Orrf! All rright ... choose sides."

They did so. Lena spun the tiny top on the counter in front of the screen. "Gimel," M'ress chortled triumphantly. "I win."

"You always win, Kit," Lena grumbled, but only briefly. After all, they had both made the cut. She punched out her name with the attendant request for information.

An ultra-rapid series of pictures blurred the screen as the desk-top brain hunted through the records. Finally, an immensely detailed chart—Lena Goldblum reduced to numerical molecules—appeared.

"One thousand eighty-three," she read from the blow-up of the bottom line.

Excellent out of ten thousand ... about average among those who would advance. And of the two thousand, only twenty percent again would graduate ... *the* Four Hundred.

"Not too good, but I have plenty of time to bring it up," she observed confidently.

"Yes, and that's betterr than—"

"And look!" Lena shouted excitedly. "I've been approved for my first request, security training!"

Two numbers, M'ress thought, that would determine their lives for the next several years. Class ranking and section. Two numbers.

"Now you, Kit."

M'ress made the request. Again the high-speed hunt, again the computer settled on the necessary card.

It was hard to say which girl was the more flabbergasted.

"M'ress," Lena gulped, "I never knew." She looked at her roommate for half a year as if she were seeing her for the first time.

There it was . . . class ranking: 0022.

"Means nothing," M'ress whispered. "Someone always has to rrank numberr one and someone has to rrank ten thousand. They'rre not absolutes . . . just rroughs. Just a convenient statistical abstrract for the administrration."

"But, M'ress . . ." Lena stopped, sensing a sudden shift in her friend's attitude. "Kit, what's wrong? Sure it's only a rough number, but even so, aren't you pleased?"

"Look." M'ress pointed to the other critical number. It translated as: COMMUNICATIONS. "I wanted Science Section," she growled bitterly. "Administrrative science with a culturral anthrro over-majorr leading to executive officerrship and eventual Captaincy."

"Practically everyone wants administration and a chance at command, Kit," said Lena comfortingly. "You know how pitifully few even get a *chance* to try for it. There's always the possibility of a field commission, though."

"In communications?" M'ress cried.

"Look, at least you've got a chance to reach the Bridge. That's a lot closer than I'll ever get. Of course, I know I would never have it upstairs for command anyway."

She forced a smile.

"Maybe the computer read some of your poetry."

M'ress had to smile at that.

"I suppose I should be thrilled even to pass on. But

I've been making rrankings like that all my life and you get to expect them afterr a while."

"This is Starfleet Academy though, M'ress," Lena reminded her. "Not some—excuse me—provincial school."

"That's so," M'ress was forced to admit. She brightened. "Yes, by the Prrey, I ought to be prroud, and excited, *mrrrr!* Ssst . . . if I have to worrk my way up thrrough communications, then it's thrrough communications I'll worrk."

"That's the spirit," encouraged Lena.

"And I'm going to keep on with my poetrry, too . . . no matter wherre it puts me in the mind of some centrral collection of solenoids and scrrews."

(Sun to Black Star . . . even!)

"M'ress . . . we've been hit, badly!"

M'ress looked up from her seat at the library viewer and stared anxiously at Ankee, the short, stocky Jarite engineering ensign who had become one of her closest companions on the heavy cruiser *Hood*. Their sections were totally different in function, as were their individual assignments; but they shared a deep and abiding interest in the construction of reform-era poetry.

Now he looked exhausted, badly battered about one side of his head, and a little scared.

"I felt a slight shudder, Ankee, but I didn't think . . . I only heard the yellow alert sound and saw no harm in continuing with this work."

"Surprise attack," he told her tiredly. "No one had time to do more than react instinctively. Not even time to sound battle stations." He added, seeing her brow furrow, "Kzinti."

"Oh, we hit back at them, all right. Knocked out both engines, from what I hear; and scuttlebutt has it she's lost a lot of atmosphere, but . . . ," he paused worriedly, "there's been no further word from the Bridge in some time."

"*What* Bridge?"

M'ress looked past Ankee as her friend turned. Lieutenant Morax was standing in the doorway, fighting to keep from shaking. Despite his three legs, the soft-voiced security officer looked none too stable.

"The Bridge is gone."

"What?" both ensigns gasped simultaneously.

"Gone," Morax continued to mutter, in a tone that hinted he still didn't accept it himself. "Just . . . gone Captain Oxley, Commander Umba, Lieutenant Commander D'Uberville . . . everybody."

"Then who's in command?" wondered M'ress. "That would leave . . ."

Morax shook his head sadly. "Chief Ellis was on the bridge, too. Which means—"

"You," Ankee put in.

"Me. Believe me, it's an honor I could do without."

"What happened?" M'ress pressed.

Morax made a complicated gesture. "The first attack. Direct hit on the Bridge by a disruptor bolt before we could get our screens up. We missed deflecting it by seconds. Too long." The security chief seemed about to cry.

"What's ourr status?" M'ress asked tightly.

"Engines disabled, Bridge gone, Fire Control scrambled to hell and gone. "We're a derelict," Morax told them. "The Kzinti's in little better shape. You know what that means."

"Open to salvage," Ankee said huskily.

M'ress had moved quickly to the tiny computer console. She cleared off her work project—three weeks' study gone, no time to mourn—ran through several shunting operations while the other two watched. She tried again, a third time, finally quit in disgust.

"I could have told you," Morax said sympathetically, "our communications are completely gone, as well."

"So," guessed Ankee, "we sit here, both ships drifting forever in space, unless by accident . . ."

"No, Ensign," Morax cut in. "The Kzinti is totally disabled from a mobility standpoint, true. Offensively, true. But our remaining backup sensory equipment indicates they are managing to put out a signal—faint, but a signal nonetheless—toward their nearest relay station.

"We're deep in Federation territory, but we might as

well be on the Galactic rim since we can't generate a similar signal. When theirs is picked up, it'll send another Kzinti warship racing here. They'll take the *Hood* in tow, after disposing of any inconvenient vermin who happen to be witnesses, of course."

"So that's it, then," cursed Ankee fatalistically, slumping in the portal. "No way of fighting back. We can't run and we can't fight—we can't even call for help. But they can."

M'ress was thinking furiously, then she asked, "What arre you going to rrecommend?"

"A great deal of prayer," Morax replied. He turned to leave.

"There's another possibility. Less spiritual, but with a betterr chance of succeeding, I think."

Morax stopped, gaped at her.

"Come now, Ensign, I . . ."

"No, rreally—if you'rre cerrtain the Kzinti communications arre still intact."

"We've got a definite indication they're putting out a signal," the security chief replied. "It will take some time to reach a Kzinti border relay post, considering the lack of power behind it. But it will reach."

"So," M'ress went on, "if we could get contrrol of that same transmitter and beam to one of *ourr* stations, a Federration vessel would get herre in half the time the nearrest Kzin could."

She waited while Ankee and Morax exchanged puzzled glances.

"I'm not sure what you're proposing, Ensign," Morax said finally, "but if it's what I think, I absolutely . . ."

She slid out of the chair, came to the door. Her words were low, urgent. "You've got no choice, 'Acting Captain Morrax.'

"We Caitains and the Kzinti sharre common genetic rroots in the farr past, as do the Vulcans and the RRomulans. With a little carreful makeup, I could pass for a Kzin. A small one, but pass I would. Communications arre my specialty. With Lieutenant Tavi gone . . . ," she swallowed stiffly, "I'm the best qualified to trry this.

"I can speak Kzin well enough to fool theirr own warr council. And the last thing they'll be expecting is a boarrding parrty of one. Now, what's ourr trransporrter capability?"

"I haven't had time to check," began Morax, "but . . ."

"Then find out, and if anything still worrks, have someone stand by to beam me aboarrd when I'm rready. If I can rreach theirr station and hold it long enough to get a single burrst off towarrd the Cetacea system . . ."

"How long," protested Ankee, "do you think you could hold such a spot against an aroused bunch of Kzinti? Against even one Kzin?"

"All I need is a couple of minutes to re-align the directional antenna—they've got to be using the dirrectional, otherrwise one of ourr patrrols might pick up theirr signal—and get off one little scrream."

"And after that?" wondered a worried Morax. "What about the chances of our beaming you back aboard when you're finished—in one piece. The odds . . ."

"Let us not exerrt ourrselves with minorr details, acting Captain," she cut in. "I don't want anyone rretrieving me until I signal back that I'm good and rready, too."

"Well," she added, when neither officer essayed anything further, "arre you both of a sudden tongueless?"

Ankee stared at the deck while Morax . . . Morax looked exceedingly unhappy.

"If there were another way, no matter how extreme or unlikely the chance of success . . . You know what the Kzinti would do to you?"

"Morre details," she snapped, but trembling inside. "As you arre well awarre, there is no other way." She started past them. "I'm going down to Recreation. Someone down therre ought to be able to make me up.

"Meanwhile, acting Captain, you might have someone go overr the interrnal schematic of a Kzinti crruiser. It won't help if I'm set down in the middle of one of theirr interrogation chamberrs."

Against all probabilities—against all hopes and prayers and reasonableness—the scheme worked.

Of course, as soon as the signal was changed and beamed out toward Federation territory, other Kzinti on board the warship got wind of what was happening.

Still, M'ress almost got away unscathed, thanks to the timely and incredibly precise manipulations of the officer manning the transporter controls.

Almost.

Fortunately, the majority of scars were correctable by surgery, the others cosmetically concealed. The cause in which they were obtained was the reason why after only two short years on active duty, Ensign M'ress was promoted to the rank of lieutenant and assigned the prestigious post of alternate communications officer on board the *U.S.S. Enterprise.*

Actually, the hardest part had not been making it through Starfleet Academy, nor had it been the deception she'd so devastatingly performed on the Kzinti.

No, the hardest part had been the steady separation from the traditionally close-knit Caitian family. She smiled to herself. Her mater had been right about her setting an example for her younger sister and brothers; all three were now serving in Starfleet in various capacities. So M'mar had learned to bear up under the honor of having not one but four kits achieve officer grade in Starfleet.

A litter of warriors and militarists, she'd raised—she often grumbled. But privately, she was proud, proud.

And her sire, M'nault, wasn't private about it.

(White Satellite to Black Sun two, plus one. Check) "Check."

M'ress blinked, looked up across the multilevel game board.

"There's a great deal on your mind, Lieutenant," observed the concerned figure seated across from her, "besides your next moves. If you wish, we can continue the game at another time."

"You'rre rright, Mrr. Spock. I wasn't concentrrating."

Spock pushed his chair back, rose. He touched a switch set in the top of the game table. The blue striping on the table rim slowly turned bright red, an indication that there was a game in suspension on it and no one should disturb the pieces.

"I do not like to pry, but your concentration was so intense—if I can do anything . . ."

"It's nothing, Mrr. Spock." She let out a deep, purring sigh. "Nothing at all, rreally. Some unimporrtant memorries, that's all."

Spock studied her skeptically, but elected not to pursue the matter any further. Not that the intimate details of M'ress' history or her mental preoccupations intrigued him so much. But as a student of intelligent behavior, he was curious as to what "minor" matters could distract an outstanding player like M'ress to the point where she would make several moves as foolish as her last.

Such a thing would never happen to him, of course.

Kirk was concluding a log entry as Spock entered the bridge. The first officer of the *Enterprise* moved to stand near the command chair, at ease and at the ready, while Kirk dictated. The captain noticed his arrival, acknowledged it with a barely perceptible nod and continued on without a break.

The subject of said log entry was currently visible on the main screen: a smallish, intensely blue-green globe. The light of a modest G-type star reflected phosphorescently back from the spines of interminable ocean. Misty cloud cover added an angelic air to the scene.

The planet's name was Argo. It was one of a surprising multitude of water worlds thus far discovered in the explored section of the Galaxy.

Argo's one peculiarity worth remarking on—and worth the *Enterprise*'s presence here—was that until quite recently (according to drone probe analysis), it had been largely a landed planet. Now its surface was ninety-seven per cent water.

No great ice caps had melted to cause this; no mythological Terran forty days and forty nights of rain had fallen. According to the data relayed back over the indifferent light-years to Starfleet Science Center by the drones, this world had been subjected to a series of evenly spaced seismic convulsions—intense without being cataclysmic—in a very brief span of time.

Forty days and forty nights of tectonic activity, perhaps. The fact that these convulsions had caused the major land masses to subside and vanish beneath the waves was not especially remarkable, Spock mused. It was the time factor which made Argo a world worth a second, more detailed look. That, and the chance that such emergence—subsidence activity might be cyclic in nature. Because there was at least one other, well-populated, world in the Federation which gave hints of being similar to Argo.

A number of techniques for dealing with such subsidings on a selective basis had been developed, but only in theory. To put them into practice would require a world like the inhabited one. Since the inhabitants of the planet in question frowned on experimentation with the planetary crust and other such intimate chunks of their home, a substitute world had to be located.

Argo was such a world . . . maybe. If so, the *Enterprise* might have a chance to try out some of those hopefully effective techniques.

Kirk wrapped up the entry, flipped off the recorder and glanced up at Spock.

As some sort of comment appeared to be in order, the Vulcan ventured, "Hardly the sort of world one would expect to be riven at any moment from core to surface, Captain."

Kirk nodded, and his gaze shifted to the screen. "No, Mr. Spock. It certainly seems placid enough on the surface. It's what's under the surface that'll be interesting. But we'll make the standard on-site survey first.

"Very good, Captain."

Kirk rose and both men started for the door.

They might, Kirk mused as the elevator took them toward the shuttle hanger, simply have beamed down with life-support belts to maintain them. The force-fields would keep them supplied with sufficient air while preventing them from drowning.

The trouble was, movement in a liquid environment while encased in a personal support field was peculiarly awkward. And mechanical transportation would be far faster.

The small door slid aside and they strode into the cavernous hangar. Two men met them by the water shuttle. One—young, brown-haired, Lincolnesque-bearded and mellow-voiced—saluted: Lieutenant Clayton, their pilot.

His companion simply smiled. "Hello, Jim. Hello, Spock."

"You're coming with us, Doctor?" asked Spock.

"No, Spock," McCoy shot back. "I'm here to evaluate the possibilities of flooding the shuttle hangar five centimeters deep so that when the shuttle departs, the water will freeze solid and we'll have the largest interstellar skating rink in existence."

Spock paused a moment, considered thoughtfully, finally observed cautiously, "You are being sarcastic again, Doctor."

"It's observational capabilities like that which make me glad that at least one competent observer is going on this trip."

"Three, actually, Doctor," Spock continued, "but we will not be offended if you come along anyway."

Kirk cut off McCoy's inevitable riposte by starting for the shuttle with the young lieutenant in tow. "Clayton?"

"Sir?"

"How long," and he gestured at the nearing craft, "since you piloted one of these?"

"It's been a while, sir," the subordinate replied readily, "but as designated shuttle pilot for this mission, I've been reviewing the appropriate tapes and techniques for the last several weeks."

Kirk muttered something inaudible, turned back before entering. "All right. Mr. Spock, Dr. McCoy . . . if you're *quite* finished?"

The long ovoid shape of the shuttle was broken only by a clear plexalloy dome set midway back on its top. One section of this was raised. A small retractable stairway led into it. Spock, McCoy and Clayton followed the captain into the crew section.

While the three senior officers settled into thickly

padded seats set into the bulkheads, Clayton eased himself into the one adjustable one that faced the instrument panel. He ignored the conversation of his superiors and concentrated instead on running a final check of the internal computer, phaser controls, and their inorganic relatives.

"Is this trip really necessary, Jim?" asked McCoy over the beeps and hums of the responding components. "Not that I'm complaining, mind. I'm tickled for the chance to get a look at another water world. Fascinating ecologies on all of them. But can't we get all the information on seismic abberations from on-board instrumentation?"

"Yes, Bones. But the regs say that any world holding life bigger than a bacterium and more complex than a coelenterate requires at least one hands-on survey by a visiting ship. It's especially necessary in this case. You know how much trouble drone probes have getting accurate data on the life of water planets."

"That's true, Jim," McCoy admitted, "even so . . ." The clear voice of Lieutenant Clayton cut him off.

"Ready, Captain."

"All right, Lieutenant, when you're set."

Clayton manipulated controls. Slowly, majestically, the two massive doors of the hangar deck began to drift apart, moving with the ease and speed of milkweed seeds in an autumn breeze. Ebony blackness speckled with brilliant pinpoints of light backed the stage. The blue-green-glowing principal performer lay below them and slightly to starboard.

The lieutenant was as good as his word—and his homework. He had a little trouble handling the entry into the atmosphere, but that was understandable. Kirk said nothing. The shuttle had been designed with underliquid maneuverability first in mind, in-flight navigability second.

Once they had penetrated the shifting cloud cover and Clayton had gotten the feel of the little ship in atmosphere, the operation grew gratifyingly smooth.

With a single exception, the surface of Argo in this region was wholly water. The shuttle skimmed low over roiling swells—all shades of blue and green that endless ocean was: azure, cerulean, deep turquoise; emerald, periodot, and flashing olivine. And where a wave crested, broke, the sea turned to amber foam flecked with white.

A strong concentration of mineral salts would be needed to stain the water that orange-brown hue— manganese, perhaps, Kirk thought.

The single exception hove into view: an island now, once the topmost crags of some mountain range. Stone exploded from the sea like a hallucinatory vision of a medieval castle. Battlements of naked basalt and porphyry offered challenge to endless legions of siege-waves, and amber moss festooned the rock-turrets with the banners of still defiant land.

Clusters of brilliant-hued shells rested in niches and crevices of the rock, and some shone phosphorescent even in the strong light of day. The amber color was prevalent here, too. It seemed to engulf the island and form a secondary atmosphere above the sea.

Not manganese then, Kirk thought. Whatever peculiar trace minerals were present here in ocean and air were likely as not alien to Earthly chemistry. He hoped the shuttle's recorder-sampler was operating at peak efficiency.

Assuredly, there was more of interest here than occasional earthquakes.

Clayton adjusted controls and the shuttle cut speed, eased downward to a damp landing. They hit gently and then slid smoothly toward the island.

They lay in the lee of the prevailing current, the island serving as shield, so here the surface was unusually smooth. As the shuttle came to a halt, Kirk and the others unfastened themselves from the protective seats.

McCoy and Spock moved to the storage lockers, started to remove the equipment they would need to properly sample what lived and was lived upon on Argo. But it was the enchanting vision of an accidental island that drew Kirk's attention.

He moved forward to stand by the busy Clayton. Through the plexalloy the jagged bastions now towering nearby resembled more than ever an impregnable repository of watery secrets. The dark shadow it cast on the otherwise unmarred ocean looked unnatural and faintly forbidding.

"Spock?"

The first officer looked over from where he was carefully constructing a small, self-powered mesh. It would skim the surface outside the shuttle for microscopic life and return automatically when full.

"Yes, Captain?"

"This is the largest remaining land mass on the planet, isn't it?"

"Yes, Captain." Spock turned back to his work, continued speaking as he fitted another part. "There are other outcroppings, but all are smaller than this. Yet according to readings taken from the ship, the ocean bottom hereabouts is fairly close to the surface. This suggests that the subsidence was unequal in places—or else we are floating above what would be regarded as a monstrously high plateau on Earth or on Vulcan. I think the irregular subsidence theory the more likely."

"I suggest," McCoy broke in, "that we stop debating theory and get down to some practical work . . . like obtaining some specimens."

"For once I agree with you, Doctor," Spock responded. Kirk smiled.

"Lieutenant Clayton, open the hatch and let our two impatient scientists get on with their business."

"Aye, sir." He reached toward the side-mounted lever which would raise the entranceway of the dome. As he did so, McCoy gestured sharply to port.

"What's that?"

"I don't see anything, Doctor," Spock said, studying the indicated spot.

"There's something in the water there," McCoy countered, beginning to feel like a mighty fool. Had he seen something or not? "There, see where the water is fountaining slightly?"

McCoy's fears of seeming a fool were put to rest by a wild churning and frothing at the indicated place. They were supplanted seconds later by more tangible fears as a brace of enormous tentacles broke the surface and hooked down like a pair of gargantuan anacondas to embrace the shuttle in a crushing grip.

Kirk was yelling something about activating the engine, but whatever had them was shaking the shuttle violently and his words were lost in the steady banging about.

Released from their protective loungers the four men tumbled about the interior like dice in a cup. There was a sudden jolt as if the ship had abruptly slammed into something hard.

Either the thing had accidentally struck a sensitive portion of itself with part of the unyielding craft or else it was generally infuriated by its inability to crack the hide of this strange prey, because it had thrown them end over end to bang to a stop against an inoffensive wave.

The shuttle automatically rolled to an upright position. Kirk then pulled himself to his feet, saw they were still seaworthy and watertight.

"Spock . . . Bones . . . Lieutenant Clayton?"

Replies came back promptly. "Surprisingly sound, Captain." "I'm all right, Jim." "Okay, I think, sir."

He stumbled to the dome, holding one hand to the large red bruise forming on his left cheek. "What was it, anyway?"

"At the moment my scientific curiosity stands in abeyance, Jim," McCoy groaned. "Just so long as it doesn't come back . . ." He struggled to his feet.

Kirk took a quick step back from the dome. "No such luck, Bones. Clayton . . ."

Before Kirk could say anything else, the upper portion of the Argoan life-form erupted from the water hard by the shuttle. From what they could see, it resembled a cross between an oversized snake and a whale, with the addition of four side-tentacles thick enough to embarrass Earth's grandfather squid. That they were fully functional had already been amply demonstrated.

It was Spock, not the more severely stunned Clayton, who slipped into the pilot's seat and edged them around in the water. He was taking action even as Kirk ordered it.

"Firing phasers on stun, Captain."

Two poles of fiery red light bolted from the nose of

the shuttle, enveloped the head of the monster in a glowing nimbus. The concentrated light danced on amber and copper colored scales.

Incredibly, the creature continued toward the shuttle for another couple of seconds. Then its continual roaring faded to an echo. Still moving weakly, reflexively, it sank from sight beneath the waves.

Uncaring swells dusted the place clean, left nothing to indicate the apparition which had loomed there moments before. Spock paused at the console a moment longer to make certain it was no ruse on the part of the monster, then moved to aid Clayton.

"It's all right, Mr. Spock." The younger officer was limping slightly. "I twisted an ankle a little, that's all. I'll be okay."

Spock nodded once, then walked to the dome to stare at the spot where the creature had disappeared. Clayton returned to his position at the front console, sitting down carefully.

"What the devil was that thing?" McCoy murmured.

As usual, the doctor gave in to his oft-times infuriating affectation for redundancy, Spock mused—and as usual, he held the easy retort in check.

"Clearly one of the multitude of life-forms which the drone survey neglected to record."

"Hard to see how something that big could be ovgrlooked," Kirk mused. "Still, with such a large area to cover in so short a time, I'm not surprised. The presence of a predator that size is a sure sign of a thriving ecology. I don't think I've ever seen anything quite like this one."

"A rough combination of Terran Cetacea and Cephalopoda, with unique characteristics of its own," Spock added.

Kirk appeared to reach a decision.

"Let's get another look at it before the stun wears off," he announced. "That was a pretty strong jolt it absorbed . . . we should be safe."

He glanced back over his shoulder.

"Submerge, Lieutenant. Keep the currents here in mind."

"Aye, sir, submerging . . ."

II

Clayton maneuvered the streamlined craft with ever greater skill. After several minutes of searching they had found no sign of the monster. But the view about the dome made up for it.

They had sunk into a green mist tinged with the ever-present amber and were now making their way through a world of green glass. The bottom here was close enough to the surface so that sunlight penetrated all the way to the sand.

If the world above with its monotonous, unvarying seascape and its looming island appeared simple and unchanging, the bottom presented a gaudy contrast.

Exotic marine flora abounded, formed a kaleidoscopic background for the alien zoo that lived in and about it. The slanting sunlight combined with an Argoal coral-analog to enhance the similarity to an Earthly topical lagoon.

Some of the ichthyoids wore broad, feathery tails that would have been more at home on a peacock than on a swimmer. And the moss which so strikingly decorated the island peaks grew even more abundantly below the surface.

Here and there schools of thousands of minute crimson fish darted in and about the densest mosses, so thick in places that the water appeared to be on fire. They reflected metallically off the polished backs of lumbering, clownish molluscs which scoured the nooks and crannies in the coral like old women at a rummage sale.

"There it is," McCoy exclaimed, even as Clayton was turning the shuttle in the direction of the somnolent sea monster. The creature had drifted slightly south of where it had gone down. Now it rested immobile on the amber sand.

20

"Look out," Kirk observed. "Try and set us down close by the head, Lieutenant."

"Yes, sir."

As the smooth metal hull settled gently into the soft bottom there was a slight grinding noise. Moss and hypnotically swaying ferns genuflected in opposite directions, while a small colony of crustaceans protested this unannounced eviction from their apartment rock with considerable verve.

Spock and McCoy adjusted their tricorders, began to take basic readings. McCoy found something which stimulated the first scientific controversy of this exploration.

"Dual respiratory system," the doctor observed. "Lungs *and* gills."

"Most odd," Spock agreed. "Unless our assumptions are correct. If land subsidence and emergence here *is* cyclic, then it would be natural for the animal population to stand ready to live in either environment.

"However, one specimen cannot be considered representative of every species on the planet. More readings of other types are essential."

"There's that amber moss, too," McCoy pointed out. "It seems to grow just as well above water as below."

The stunned monster chose that moment of temporary disinterest on the part of its bipedal observers to stir slightly. Its tentacles quivered, disturbing the sand. Abruptly, the gigantic tail jerked spasmodically.

The glancing blow was powerful enough to send the shuttle tumbling across the sea bottom, to come to a stop against a sand hill. Amber rain fell on the plexalloy dome as the displaced sand settled back toward the bottom.

A groggy Kirk decided that this particular specimen reacted a mite too unpredictably for casual study. A second stun burst as strong as the first might kill it, anything less prove ineffectual.

As Kirk stared out the dome, the monster momentarily seemed to have developed eight tentacles instead of four. And two heads. Also, there were two Spocks and two McCoys pulling themselves to their feet.

However many limbs the creature possessed, at the

moment all of them were moving in furious motion as it fought to regain its internal balance.

"Take us up, Lieutenant, it's coming around, and I think we'd better be elsewhere when it does." Clayton nodded.

The shuttle angled upward, rose from the sand and started toward the island. Kirk had one final glimpse of the beast, still thrashing about aimlessly, before the angle of ascent cut off his view.

Any normal creature, having received such a pounding, would have escaped as its first thought. This inhabitant of Argo, however, was used to running from nothing, except perhaps a larger one of its own kind. Its flailing quelled for a moment ... then the creature rolled over with a weird whistling roar and shot off with incredible speed in pursuit of the rising shuttle.

Melting greenness gave way to blue sky and a view of the island dead ahead. Expecting to see nothing but calm water, Kirk looked out the rear of the dome. And as expected, the surface rolled on unbroken—until the father of geysers erupted almost on top of them, the burst sending the nose of the shuttle slamming forward and down. It bobbed up like a cork.

Kirk had had enough of maintaining concern for nonsapient alien life-forms. "Prepare to fire phasers ..."

Spock moved to the console, adjusted the proper controls, leaving Clayton free to steer the craft. He snapped a hurried look at Kirk when a certain critical light failed to wink on as expected.

"Phasers do not respond, Captain. Obviously we have sustained some damage from being struck below."

Relief or no relief, he still should have ordered a check as a matter of course, Kirk cursed. Too late for recriminations. He looked back again, hoping that the monster had perhaps lost interest or gained satisfaction.

Instead, he saw that the hunter had moved off, turned, and was now rushing back at them, mouth agape and wide as the corridor of an underground transportation system.

"Lift off, Mr. Clayton, now!"

The lieutenant worked the proper instruments,

paused as if shot, ran through the sequence again twice as fast before throwing Kirk an anguished look.

"No response, sir! Propulsion units have been cracked . . . I'm not registering a thing."

That cavern of a gullet was drawing closer and closer. Stalactites and stalagmites of polished amber ivory lined its roof and floor.

Kirk didn't waste time on shuttle communications. If both phasers and lift engine were out, chances were bad for the more delicate beam transmitter to have survived. He used his pocket communicator.

"Kirk to *Enterprise*—red alert!"

Engineer Scott's voice reflected the urgency in Kirk's own.

"*Enterprise*, Scott speaking—what is it, Captain?"

"We're under attack, Scotty, emergency—beam us aboard." His last words were drowned in the thunderous bellow which erupted from the monster's throat.

"Full ahead, Mr. Clayton . . . !" The lieutenant hit controls, but not fast enough; the great tentacled head rose up, up, blotting out sun and sky—then came down. Kirk barely had time to grab for a hold before the gargantuan skull slammed into the shuttle.

Another deafening howl penetrated the dome and it grew dark as two huge jaws closed on the aft section of the tiny vessel.

Despite various grips, the impact sent everyone sprawling. Part of the upper jaw came down on the plexalloy dome. The transparent molding was incredibly strong, but its designers had never meant it to take this kind of pressure. It finally cracked.

Shaking the shuttle like an infuriated mastiff with a piece of meat, the monster banged it against a rocky protrusion lying just under the surface. That finished the remainder of the dome. Another shake sent shards of dome, torn internal components, and McCoy and Clayton flying.

The interior was a shambles. High-impact seats were twisted like licorice sticks. Spock lay jammed between the pilot's chair and the base of the control console, and Kirk was entangled in the remnants of some restraining straps.

Both men were unconscious, their limp forms bent and loose. But they didn't come free as the creature swam off, still battering at its stubborn prey.

"We've lost contact, Captain, a tinny voice yelled from somewhere within a maze of twisted metal. "We've lost contact. Come in, Captain, come in! Spock . . . !"

McCoy let out a whoosh as he broke the surface, looked around fearfully. But the only struggling form he saw was weak and small. He gave Clayton some support, helped him clear the water from his lungs.

Together they stared at the distant but still visible form of the monster, the cylindrical shape of the shuttle still clutched tightly in its tentacles . . . what was left of it. Even as they watched, the creature rolled over on its back and vanished beneath the waves.

McCoy tried to shout, call, but couldn't manage the breath. Once more the water was calmed, once more the distant island the only projection above the gentle swells. The shuttle, the monster . . . Kirk and Spock . . . all gone.

Hopefully they had been thrown free, probably in the other direction. As he and Clayton had been—oh, hopefully!

As McCoy was about to suggest they start searching, a not-so-alien mist distorted his vision and he experienced a brief sensation of falling.

Once the feeling had passed, he found himself standing in the main transporter chamber of the *Enterprise*, staring at the distant forms of Scott and Transporter Chief Kyle across the room. There was the sound of flesh meeting plastic alongside him, and he turned to help the fallen Clayton. Scott was there in a second to assist him.

"What happened, Bones?" But before McCoy could form a reply the chief had turned and was calling back to Kyle, "Call Sick Bay, have them get a team up here double-time!" He gazed back into the transporter alcove.

"The captain, and Mr. Spock . . ." His voice faded as he saw the look on McCoy's face.

"I didn't know . . . for certain, Scotty. We were tak-

ing readings on the local version of a sea serpent and
. . . we got a little careless. It's reaction-recovery time
. . . phenomenal . . ." A hand ran through hair matted
with amber salts. He was aware he probably sounded
as tired as Clayton looked.

"It attacked instinctively—wrong bedamned instinct!
Threw the shuttle around like a toy. A previous attack
had rendered the phasers and lift engine inoperable,
but we didn't find that out until too late. I don't know
if we could have outrun it on the surface anyway. That
thing was *fast*." He took a few steps, found out how
tired he really was and sat down at the edge of the alcove.

"I don't know what's happened to the captain or
Spock. I hope they got thrown free like Clayton and
myself."

"I'll get a search party together immediately," Scott
announced. McCoy was too exhausted to do more than
nod.

Planetary ocean stretched unbroken to infinity. Only
an occasional curl of foam turning in on itself broke
the translucent evenness.

That, and a small slim boat of silver. A small slim
boat which had been plying the surface of Argo for
some time now, plying zig-zag and spiral routes across
computer-suggested courses.

The narrow silhouette was broken only by a pair of
compact powerpacks attached to its stern . . . and three
irregular shapes seated within.

McCoy and Clayton stood in the bow, patiently
scanning the horizon with telescopic binoculars. The
doctor paused to rub his tired eyes, something he was
doing with increasing frequency.

He stopped, stared at the dappled surface without
the aid of the mounted telefocals. "Five days and we've
found nothing. *Nothing*."

"They can't just have dropped out of sight, sir," said
a sanguine Clayton. McCoy turned to eye him sadly,
shook his head.

"Currents, scavengers, a little shift in the lie of the

bottom . . ." He shrugged. "They're gone, that's all
there is to it."

Clayton said nothing and both men turned their gaze
back to the telefocals. It was the lieutenant's turn next
to break the silence.

"I see something, anyway. Barely above sea level,
bearing thirty, forty degrees to starboard, about three
kilometers off, I'd say." He fiddled with the fine adjustment on the precision focals as McCoy turned his own
glasses in the indicated direction. Clayton's voice rose.

"There's something on them catching the sun—and I
don't think it's rocks!"

All the exhaustion had gone from McCoy's eyes
now. His gaze was surgeon sharp. Scott had moved to
stare through his own set, rest turn or no.

A dark mass of cracked, tumbled boulders, worn
smooth by the constant wave action. The highest point
on the low-lying island rose barely two or three meters
from the water. McCoy pressed the telescopic switch,
and the image jumped nearer.

Details revealed odd-shaped fragments of reflective
material . . . bits of the hull and cabin section of the
lost shuttle, for sure. They lay displayed on the rocks
like ornaments on a tree.

McCoy lurched slightly as the boat shifted, lost his
gaze. Scott was swinging the prow around. He gunned
the twin power-packs and they jetted toward the rocks.

"Any sign of them, Bones?" the chief engineer
shouted as he nosed the gig into a notch between two
protruding rocks. McCoy shook his head. Clayton
scrambled out with a rope in one hand, secured it
around a projecting knob of worn obsidian that looked
solid enough to anchor the *Enterprise* itself. Clearly,
this island had not appeared within the last couple of
days.

McCoy climbed out of the gig. Ignoring the debris
strewn around his feet, he started for the peak of the
little islet, picking his path carefully around sharp edges
of metal, plastic and volcanic glass.

No doubt about it, though, the bulk of the shuttle
had been washed up—or tossed up—here. He topped
the gentle rise and looked down the other side.

That's when he spotted Kirk and Spock.

On the other side of the islet the water was barely a meter deep, washing up over amber-white sand into a miniature bay. The motionless forms of the *Enterprise*'s captain and first officer lay face down in the sand.

"They're here!" he yelled back. "Hurry!"

Seconds later Clayton and Scott were splashing through the water, dragging in panic at the two bodies.

"You think they're still alive, Bones?" Scott didn't look at his friend as he said it.

McCoy's reply was grim, honest. "Not if they've been down there for five days."

Both forms seemed to weigh tons. They fought to move Kirk to the nearest dry land while keeping his head above water.

"They might have swum here, crawled ashore dazed, and just fallen into the water recently from weakness, "McCoy said wishfully. *"Very* recently, I hope."

They finally managed to drag Kirk's waterlogged form onto a flat section of island. Leaving his feet dangling in the water, they went back for Spock.

As soon as both men were lying alongside one another, McCoy reached into his backpack and removed the medical tricorder. Adjusting it quickly, he passed it over Kirk's chest, then reset it and did the same with Spock. Then he made additional adjustments and repeated the action, including head and neck this time.

While Scott and Clayton looked on anxiously, McCoy studied the resultant readouts. Without a word, he ran through the entire sequence again, finally sat back and frowned at the instrument as though it had suddenly grown arms and legs.

"For the sake of Reaction, say somethin'!" Scott eventually exploded. "Are they alive?"

McCoy blinked, appeared to come out of a dream. He looked at Spock without seeing him—then ran through the examination yet another time.

"Their life systems are still functioning," he finally said, as Scott was about to scream. "Metabolism is slowed, heartbeat slightly faster, all other bodily functions altered—but within acceptable parameters." He looked up in confusion.

"I say 'acceptable' because they're incontrovertably alive. But there's something about their lungs and the rest of their respiratory systems I can't figure at all." He shook the tricorder. "Not with this toy, anyway."

Clayton interrupted, gestured at the bodies. "They're coming around."

Kirk's eyes opened first . . . opened, and opened, until they stared skyward in shock and fear. He grabbed at his throat, and his words came out in a feathery, agonized whisper as he twisted on the damp stone.

"Can't . . . breathe. Suffocating . . . !"

"No . . . air . . . choking . . . odd . . ." Spock said huskily, like a dying asthmatic.

All three officers stared at their two comrades in horror: helpless, confused, uncertain. Spock's hands went to his chest in a reflexive spasm, Kirk's shifting between chest and throat. Both men began tearing at their shirts, the actions of someone fighting to clear some invisible constriction from his lungs.

That was when McCoy first noticed the fine membrane stretched between their fingers. It looked organic, not artificial—almost like webbing, in fact. And that slight, silvery-amber flaking on the backs of Kirk's hands . . . why, it was as if the captain had grown scales!

"Help . . . !" Kirk whispered hoarsely, "Can't . . . breathe . . ."

"What's happening to them, Bones?" Scott pleaded. "What's goin' on?"

"Something's changed their whole respiratory structure," McCoy whispered in awe. "They can't live in the atmosphere anymore. Not a gaseous one, anyway." He stood, grabbed Kirk's arms. "Get his ankles! Help me get them back in the water!"

They had an easier time wrestling the two men back into the shallow pool than they had had pulling them out. As soon as their faces passed beneath the clear surface, both men ceased struggling. Instead of grabbing at their chests, they relaxed completely.

McCoy stared in disbelief, even though he half expected what would happen, as Kirk rolled over on the sand and stared up at him through the crystal-clear surface. As to which officer was the more shocked, no one could say.

Scott walked over to stand next to him, likewise gazing down at his two good friends in horrified fascination.

"What do we do now, Doctor?" McCoy hesitated, then turned to the chief engineer and spoke with conviction.

"We get the captain and Mr. Spock on board, Scotty." And he went on to outline what had to be done.

The corridor was empty except for McCoy. The security chambers in Sick Bay were used (infrequently, at that) for the care and treatment of criminals or dangerous aliens. Now one of them had been converted to a much different—and more vital—use. McCoy would encounter no one as he spoke into the recording pickup.

"Medical log, Stardate 5527.1 Captain Kirk and First Officer Spock were rescued—with qualifications—forty-eight hours ago."

He turned the last corner into the recently empty chamber. In place of the double-security door just inside the entrance, a rather different restraining wall had been installed. It consisted of a plate of clear plexalloy, backed by an air space, and then another plexalloy plate. Beyond this airtight seal the chamber was filled four-fifths full with water—a special kind of water, at that.

McCoy was taking no chances with substitutions from the *Enterprise*'s own tanks. The water which filled the room had been transported up in containers from the Argoan world-ocean—from the inlet where Kirk and Spock had been found. The amber sand that covered the floor of the room came from the same location. McCoy's only liberty had been with the air supply: he had to substitute a pump for the natural plant oxygenation system below. So far, neither officer had demonstrated any ill effects from this one concession to convenience.

Kirk and Spock were at the far end of the room,

moving aimlessly, dispiritedly over the bottom sand. They were deep enough in thought, undoubtedly musing on their present situation, so that they failed to notice the doctor's entrance. McCoy studied them, resumed speaking into the pickup.

"They have no recollection of what happened after they were thrown from the shuttle. Medical analysis has revealed the presence of an unknown and as yet unidentified substance in their bloodstreams. There is a high probability that this substance is responsible for the alteration of their metabolism and for changing them into water-breathers."

He stopped, shut the recorder off. Both men had noticed his arrival and were moving toward the transparent wall. As they approached, McCoy once again marveled at the process which had somehow altered his friends' internal structure so efficiently.

Even their eyes had been affected. They were now covered with a transparent film like the second eyelids of some lizards. And of course there were the primary manifestations of the change such as the pronounced scaling and toughening of the skin, increased layers of subcutaneous fatty tissue, and webbing of fingers and toes.

While the two officers stared at him mutely, he moved to a panel set in the wall, examined the gauges and meters it proffered.

Temperature, pressure, salinity, oxygen content . . . everything read normal . . . for a fish. He nodded to the watching Kirk and Spock. Kirk acknowledged with a single jerk of his head and McCoy touched a switch in the bottom of the panel.

A metal section in the nontransparent portion of the wall slid aside. McCoy entered the pressure cubicle and touched another switch, closing the door behind him. A nudge on the belt at his waist, and the glow of a life-support system enveloped his form in soft yellow radiance.

At the adjustment of a simple lever set inside the cubicle, water began to creep up around his feet, ankles, knees. When the chamber was completely filled,

McCoy slid the interior door aside and walked clumsily into the water room.

Kirk and Spock were waiting for him. As usual, their voices held a slight fuzziness, like a beam transmission coming in unamplified from across too many light-years. That they sounded even halfway normal was in itself remarkable, but whatever had touched them had been thorough . . . their vocal cords had been altered for speaking under water.

"Well, Bones?" was all Kirk said.

"We're stumped, Jim. Nothing's worked. We've pretty much settled on this new hormone in your blood as the root cause of the entire mutation. Antidote doesn't automatically follow identification, however. There are some of the weirdest-looking molecules involved you ever saw, and they go on forever. So far the situation defies analysis."

Kirk just nodded—there wasn't much else he could do. "What about the other thing . . . are you sure the alteration wasn't performed naturally?"

McCoy shook his head. "No, Jim. Someone's been working on the both of you. I'm certain of that. There are too many signs of penetration at key structural points—you had to receive the hormone artificially."

Kirk let out a bitter, bubbling laugh. "Bang goes the theory of there being no intelligent life on Argo." He paused, thoughtfully. "The medical computers have the entire medicinal knowledge of the Federation in their archives. Can't you duplicate the procedure on a lab animal, then work backwards to find the antidote?"

McCoy didn't mention the nagging fear that the mutation might be irreversible. "Sorry, Jim. The surgico-chemical methodology here is utterly alien to us—to me, anyhow. Highly sophisticated, too. If I knew how to begin to approach the procedure, I might . . ." His voice trailed off.

"So we are left with locating a previously unknown, unsuspected sapient life-form below," Spock put in. "Evidently the initial surveys saw nothing but simple marine forms." McCoy looked hesitant.

"I don't see how even a dumb drone could miss a race capable of this kind of medical technology."

"Medical technology is not highly visible," Spock countered. "Knowledge of that sort does not imply knowledge of, for example, advanced structural engineering or other highly visible signs of civilization. Many primitive cultures possess basic, yet complex medical abilities."

"You're reaching, Spock," said McCoy.

"It is only one of several possible explanations," the first officer readily admitted. "Another lies in the composition of the Argoan sea itself. The presence of large amounts of dissolved metals and mineral salts could easily distort delicate sensor readings, block others entirely. Also, such sensors were probably set for shallow scans, ignoring possibly inhabited depths."

McCoy smiled.

"All very plausible, Spock. But if true, where does that leave us? We can't carry out efficient underwater exploration without the aqua-shuttle, and that was our only vehicle designed for liquid-environment study." He gestured at the belt circling his waist.

"We can exist underwater with life-support belts, but out time is limited and our mobility even more so. Also, if there's somebody down there who wants to stay hidden, it would be pretty damn difficult to hide a bunch of floating yellow light bulbs."

"Well, *we* aren't limited!" Kirk blurted in frustration. "Spock and I go anywhere in that ocean as efficiently as the natives." He smiled grimly. "We've been designed to do so."

McCoy's face took on a look of alarm. "Too risky, Jim. Argo is totally unexplored. If sensors couldn't penetrate that metalized soup you want to go swimming about in, chances are communications won't be much good, either. And if there are any more minnows down there like the one that hit the shuttle . . ."

Kirk's smile widened, but the grimness remained in his voice. "We don't have a choice, Bones." He waved a webbed hand. "I can't command a ship from in here . . . hell, I can't even *live* in here! We'd go crazy in a week!"

"The captain somewhat exaggerates the subjective time involved," Spock corrected evenly, "but the inevitability of his prediction is one I'm not prepared to argue with."

"I know how you feel, Jim, Spock," said McCoy. "But there's still a chance we might find a solution in the lab. If you go down into that ocean, out of contact ..." Kirk cut him off.

"Right now the percentages give us two choices, Bones. Live in an aquarium for the rest of our lives like curiosities, freaks—or stay on Argo as her first Federation settlers. I refuse to accept either one of them."

McCoy shifted his attention from the stubborn set of Kirk's face to appeal to Spock.

"What about you, Spock? You can view this in a logical, dispassionate manner."

"The captain states the case emotionally, of course," Spock replied instantly, "but correctly." McCoy's expression fell. "I would be of very little value to this ship—or to myself—if I were to remain confined to a tank in Sick Bay." He paused, added, "In a way, we are total invalids, Doctor. Something you should be able to understand. We must seek any possible treatment, no matter what the corollary dangers."

Kirk raised his right hand, studied the webbing. "Any intelligence that can produce this kind of mutation ought to be able to change us back. *Has* to change us back." He lowered the hand and stared unwaveringly at McCoy.

"There are some other physicians in this vicinity, Bones, and we've *got* to find them ..."

III

The sun of Argo, slightly yellower than Sol, glinted sharply off mirrorlike swells, struck the small silver splinter excitedly and raced on to illumine the island.

Kirk, Spock, Scott and Clayton filled the gig, the latter two holding phasers as they surveyed the surrounding surface for signs of anything even faintly inimical. The tiny boat bobbed just outside the long morning shadows cast by the towering island.

Kirk and Spock made final adjustments of the dark green vinyl that clung to their bodies like a second skin. Bubbles burst occasionally inside the awkward, water-filled masks they wore. Spock moved to the side of the gig while Kirk turned to face his chief engineer. His words came through the mask barely comprehensible.

"We'll make contact as soon as possible, Mr. Scott."

"Aye, sir," Scott replied uneasily. He felt no better about this than had McCoy.

Kirk moved to the side of the gig, looked at his first officer. Spock nodded once. Both men took a deep breath, the water level falling visibly within their faceplates. Then they hurriedly removed both masks and attendant tanks, dropped them into the boat, and dove over the side.

Scott moved to the side, looked down at both men floating comfortably just under the surface. Kirk looked up at him, waved once, and turned to swim downward. The water was clear and Scott continued staring for a long time, until both men had finally disappeared from view . . .

There are three habitable zones to most life-giving worlds: the air, the land and, lastly, the sea. And those who have claimed either of the first two have clearly not deigned to get their feet wet.

34

It's not merely the incredible lushness that mesmerizes those who plow beneath the surface, nor is it the overwhelming abundance of life that comprises such lushness. To most, it's the constant motion that contrasts so heavily with the stilted, jointed world of air-breathers. Everything underwater is part of a single, unending ballet—a dancing ecology, where every inhabitant from the lowliest worm or plant to the bemuscled and fanged carnivore knows its assigned steps and performs uncomplainingly a perpetual choreography.

Such was the world of green glass through which Kirk and Spock now probed a leisurely path. Descending gradually, they leveled off about a dozen meters from the sandy bottom, began to swim outward from the island. Clusters of amber moss sequined with phosphorescent shells and tiny crawling things drifted lazily in the gentle current. Tight formations of brilliantly hued little fish wheeled and spun in Prussian cloudlets, while larger solitary swimmers observed enviously.

The two bipeds began to move in a widening spiral, now well out from the lonely gig bobbing far above and behind them. Finally, on the fourth curve out, Kirk and Spock encountered what looked very much like a cultivated area. The garden was laid out in an unearthly but undeniably artificial fashion. Instead of distinct rows of different plants, all grew together, but neatly spaced among themselves. There was no crowding, no competition for light or sandy soil among the green, pink and amber vegetation.

Climbing over low sand dunes, the garden appeared to thicken in the distance. A few kicks brought Kirk and Spock to the outlying growths. Wordless, they examined the unmistakable signs of hand planting, constant weeding and care. Spock pointed and without a word they swam to the top of the first dune. They gently nudged through the dense vegetation crowning its top and studied the view beyond.

The garden, farm, or whatever it was stretched out impressively, occupying the sandy plain in all directions for a considerable distance. Far more commanding, however, were the shapes that swam slowly and purposefully among the intricate patterns.

They were humanoid and had almost human fore-limbs. But the rear limbs bore no resemblance to any-thing mankind had ever possessed. The legs appeared almost boneless, while the feet were true flippers, sup-ple and flexible. A small dorsal fin set just back of the neck between the shoulder blades added to the alien as-pect. The skin was a variant of the omnipresent amber, with shades of gold or green, while strands of vestigial hair the color of silver and gold tinsel topped the skull.

The race was obviously mammalian, women mixing in about equal numbers with men in the garden. Both sexes were clad in close-fitting garments of minute, metallically colored shells arranged in a multitude of individual designs.

"Once again, the basic humanoid model dominates," Spock murmured softly, "fully adapted for oceanic sur-vival."

"Even so, Spock, they still seem to retain some above-water movements. Maybe instinctive, maybe habitual ... I don't know. Here's another sign of the rapid subsidence of land hereabouts." He paused. "And I think we've been noticed."

Sure enough, several heads had turned to stare in their direction. Some of the figures were moving hastily backward, giving signs of alarm.

"I cannot vouch for their other senses," Spock com-mented appraisingly, "but their hearing is evidently acute."

"Well, we came to find them," Kirk sighed. He kicked with both legs, moving through the soft growth and down the slope. Spock followed.

At this first hint of movement, several more of the Argoans moved away, while others stood their ground and brandished tools which were none the less lethal-looking for all their agricultural design. One of the na-tives drifted slightly in front of his companions, then mouthed something momentarily incomprehensible at Kirk and Spock. Apparently the linguistic pattern was relatively standard. The tiny universal translators strapped beneath the green bodysuits hummed softly and the message came out in their ear speakers as, "Go away, air-breathers. You are not wanted here."

Kirk had hoped for a friendly greeting at best, a curious one at the least. But this expression of familiarity combined with hostility had taken him aback.

Keeping his gaze on the speaker, he directed his voice toward the pickup set in the concealed translator. It rescrambled his voice into something the sea-dwellers could comprehend.

"We won't harm you . . . we are friends. We seek only friendship . . . and knowledge."

"Leave us!" a woman shouted from the crowd. "It is enough for our young to have saved your lives once. If you go on, nothing will save you again." She turned, swam with powerful strokes over the next dune.

Others turned, started to follow. "Wait, listen," Kirk implored those departing, "we only . . ."

"Go away!" the man at the head of the mob shouted. He lingered longer than the others; but eventually he, too, turned and swam furiously to catch up.

A mystified Kirk and Spock found themselves floating alone in the field.

"It doesn't make any sense, Spock. They said that they saved us once; and so they have, but why . . . ?"

"Excuse me, Captain," Spock cut in, "but I believe their exact phrasing was, 'our young saved your lives once.'" That gave Kirk pause.

"Yes, that's right—and these adults didn't seem to approve." He stared in the direction taken by the vanished Argoans. "The answers appear to be that way, Mr. Spock."

As they swam after the retreating farmers, Spock mused, "They are not particularly rational," he observed in a mildly reproving tone, "or at least one of them would surely have realized that we were badly outnumbered as well as apparently weaponless.

"Yet even so, they were frightened. Their primitive fear of air-breathers and this," he gestured around them, "evidence of simple hand farming hardly indicate a race capable of highly advanced surgical procedures. A curious dichotomy here, Captain. Our observations will not readily supply a solution."

"Then we'll just have to press a little harder, Spock.

Eventually something's going to have to give. With answers, I hope." They swam on in silence.

Several minutes of steady swimming brought them to the base of a coral-studded reef which rose to the surface. Kirk treaded water easily as they studied the sweeping escarpment. It swept off unbroken to left and right.

"Surely they didn't go over the top of this, Spock."

"Possible but not likely, Captain, I agree. I suggest we separate and study potential approaches, staying within sight of one another."

"All right." Kirk swam off to the left, Spock went the other way. Soon thereafter, he turned at a feathery yell from his first officer.

"Here, Captain . . . !"

A moment later he drifted alongside Spock, where the latter floated by a crevice in the undersea palisade—a fathomless, gaping wound that penetrated the reef for an unknown distance.

"Excellent place for an ambush," he muttered.

"True, Captain. Yet why arrange so elaborate a deception? They could easily have overpowered us earlier. I submit they went through here . . . without stopping." He nodded toward the horizontal shaft.

Both men worked at their suit belts, produced thin, sealed cylinders—powerful undersea lights. Kirk activated his, turned to throw a tubular beam of brightness into the crack. He moved it around, and the beam revealed nothing but naked rock, dead coral, and a few stunted plants and some terrified dwellers in darkness, who quickly darted out of sight into private abysses of their own.

Keeping both beams fairly parallel, they entered the trench.

It was longer than Kirk expected. In places it became almost a tunnel, as the walls arched overhead to blot out all hints of the surface.

He forced himself to concentrate on the finite cone of rock illuminated by the light. This was a place for observation, not imagination, to hold sway.

Something touched him on the shoulder and he jerked sharply, but relaxed when he found it was only

Spock's hand. The first officer extinguished his light, motioned for Kirk to do the same. They waited silently while their eyes readjusted to the absence of light. Or *was it* absent?

For several moments while they floated in dark coolness, he saw nothing. Then he became aware that he could make out the faint outlines of the trench around them, albeit dimly.

The illumination appeared to emanate from somewhere close ahead. A few kicks brought them into increased light from overhead once again. Eventually they reached the end of the trench.

Here the coral rampart dropped off in a steep cliff to a broad sandy plain deeper and wider than the one they'd just left. What rose lofty and ethereal there made the manicured gardens and jeweled schools of fish they'd seen pale to insignificance.

What they had come upon was an underwater city, constructed with complete disregard for any ancient cataclysm, any present currents, any concern of any sort save aesthetics . . . a metropolis of faery.

Thin winding towers emulated the internal configuration of spiral seashells in grace and strength. Another huge, shell-shaped structure dominated the city, rising in its center. It was as if the city had been poured whole, entire, from a single, carefully sculpted mold, instead of being built by piece and bit.

At the point nearest the base of the coral cliff, a large archway formed a prominent break in the wall that surrounded the city. Variously clad inhabitants were swimming in and out in a steady two-way stream, intent on unknown aspects of Argoan commerce.

"Beautiful . . . and fascinating," Spock commented. "Notice the wall and use of the archway, when both are easily avoidable. Both carry-overs from land-dwelling times."

"All the more reason to wonder, Spock," said Kirk, shaking his head in puzzlement. "A civilization capable of building something like this, able to withstand continental subsiding, capable of medical accomplishments unheard of in the Federation—why should they be afraid of us, Spock?"

"Perhaps the proper term would be abhorrence, Captain, not fear. It is quite possible they find us grotesque and ugly. Basis enough for their reactions thus far. There is ample precedent in Earth's history."

Kirk nodded slowly. "Agreed. Still, we've got to get inside, no matter what they think of our features. There seems to be much less activity on the far side." Spock strained his gaze.

"I also feel no cultural inhibitions about ignoring the archway, Captain."

Dodging occasional solitary Argoans and taking care to remain a good distance from the city proper, the two men began to swim in a broad curve away from what they'd determined to be the city's main entrance.

Eventually they approached a section of wall that looked deserted. Even so, they felt conspicuous against the bright white and amber sand bottom. They waited until the lowing sun formed a dark shadow behind one thick tower, then swam for it.

A quick survey revealed they were in a little frequented section of the city. Kirk motioned and they swam slowly toward its center. He had no definite plan in mind—there was nothing to formulate one on—only that they had to contact the physician-scientists who had instigated the initial mutation. Persuasion would hopefully follow.

They made rapid progress, keeping close to the walls of low-lying structures wherever feasible. Once they almost kicked head-on into a crowd of busy Argoans as they stumbled into a central crossway. They had to dart back into a nook between buildings and wait for the aliens to pass.

"There it is," Kirk finally whispered.

They were floating on the opposite side of a broad, open plaza from the huge shell-shaped central structure. Right now it was devoid of strollers, and both officers wondered at the absence of citizens.

"Perhaps everyone is out in the fields at this time," Spock speculated, "or deep within the structures engaged in daily tasks we cannot conceive of. Or it may be that . . ."

Words and actions were cut off abruptly as a large

weighted net dropped neatly over them. Two males appeared on either side and above them, crossed in a deadly precision maneuver beneath the two startled officers and pulled the net tight.

Kirk and Spock found themselves unable to get a purchase on anything solid, unable to get any speed in the folds of the net, and unable to break it. All the while they were discovering these depressing facts, their captors were towing them efficiently toward the very domed edifice they'd sought to reach.

Kirk finally stopped fighting the netting and relaxed. They might need their strength later and have a better chance to use it. He also tried to look on the bright side of things.

They had wanted to enter the shell-shaped building—very well, it seemed they were going to do that. Not as stealthily as he had planned, perhaps, but half an apple was better than none.

They entered through a broad, low, open arch much like the anachronistic city gate, were towed through several twisting, winding halls. Inside, at least, the Argoans had managed to shuck off enough of their land-based memory to build without regard to land-based gravity.

Some of the hallways dipped up in curves, others ran down to undisclosed depths at crazy angles. Eventually they emerged into a huge auditorium near the roof of the building. As they did so Kirk realized why they had seen so few Argoans swimming over the rooftops.

Most of the buildings were doubtless arranged like this one, with transparent or translucent roofs to let in the light of day. Mass movement overhead would not only be disconcerting, it would block the light as well as eliminate privacy.

Kirk then turned his attention to more immediate matters. The chamber walls were decorated with huge globes of a creamy, pearl-like luster. There was a raised dais at the far end of the chamber. Its three carved seats were occupied by male Argoans.

It was difficult to judge age with any accuracy. But judging from their attitude and bearing as much as outward appearance, Kirk felt these three were fully mature specimens. One was slim and appeared to be regarding them with a thoughtful, though amused air. The one on the far right was slightly paunchy, and his expression was less readable. Between them, the tallest of the triumvirate studied Kirk with piercing amber eyes that seemed to cut right through him. A remarkable personality, Kirk decided instantly, and the one to be watched most carefully.

There was a lower dais set to the left, again with three seats. Two of its occupants were males, the third female—attractive in a fishy sort of way. They were generally little smaller than the other three. But their motions were quicker, their eyes moved faster, and Kirk had the definite impression that they were considerably younger than those sitting on the main platform.

Time for analysis vanished as Kirk found himself tumbling head over heels toward the dais, net and all. He thrashed about, trying to regain his balance in the enclosed space.

"Here are the spies, Tribune," the translator reported in his ear—the words of one of their captors. There was an unmistakable hint of disgust in his final words: "Air-breathers!"

The tall one, the one with the eyes, rose from the dais to hover in the water before them. He studied Kirk and Spock coldly, and the translator managed to convey some of that coldness across unemotional circuitry.

"You stand."

"Inaccurate," mumbled Spock, struggling to turn erect within the clinging coils of the net.

"I am Domar," their questioner began, "the High Tribune of the . . ."

"Aquans" was the nearest the translator could come to interpreting the unpronounceable name these folk had for themselves.

"These are my advisors, Cadmar and Cheron," the imposing speaker continued, indicating the beings to his right and left.

Kirk gave up trying to extricate himself from the net, settled for striking a dignified post within. "I am Captain James Kirk of the Starship *Enterprise*. This is my first officer, Mr. Spock."

The thin brows of the High Tribune drew together uncertainly. "Your words are meaningless. You are air-breather enemies from the surface. We have been expecting you for a long time, never letting down our guard from the Old Days."

"If you find my words meaningless, I confess I find yours confusing, Tribune," Kirk admitted truthfully. "We came here in peace."

Domar's frown deepened. His two companions gazed grimly at the officers. "The ancient records," he announced, "warn that air-breathers never come in peace."

"Are you saying," broke in a new, challenging voice, "that they come in war, then ... without any weapons?"

Kirk looked sharply to his left. The young female was on her flippers, staring belligerently at the Tribune. On her right side one of the males added, "Can we do nothing without consulting the ancient records? Have we no ability to analyze and decide without the advice of the long-dead?"

Obviously this was a very different society from, say, that of Earth; for this challenge produced definite hints of hesitation in the attitudes of two of the Tribunes—Cadmar and Cheron. One minute they appeared as inflexible as the walls of the city, the next and their convictions showed cracks at the first objection from their younger colleagues. If the High Tribune Domar felt the same lack of assurance, he didn't show it.

There was an unmistakable weariness in Cheron's voice as he countered, "Why do the Junior Tribunes always wish to change the records? Are the words of those who built this city empty for them? Are they ... ?"

Domar put out a quieting hand, then the council leader turned and made a gesture to the two guards.

"Let the mesh be removed—but stand ready. Beware the air-breather's deceptiveness."

With considerable relief, Kirk and Spock felt the netting being removed. As they were freed, all six Tribunes inspected them with renewed interest. The powerful amplifier in the tiny translator brought Kirk a whispered translation from—he struggled to recall the vaguely Greco-Roman sounding names. Lemas—that was the youngster's name.

"The surgeons did their jobs well," he was murmuring. "Observe the perfection of the metamorphosis and the ease with which their bodies have adapted."

Kirk felt faintly flattered—the sort of mild exhilaration one experiences when participating in the hard-won success of others. Still, the Tribune's words were not conclusive evidence. The process still might have been initiated naturally and only completed by artificial means. It would pay to be sure.

His natural inclination was to address himself immediately to the younger, seemingly friendly Tribunes. He needed his years of diplomatic experience to tell himself that their elders wouldn't look kindly on the implied slight. So he directed his first words to Domar.

"Then your scientists *did* induce these mutations in our systems?"

"We had no other moral choice. Unlike air-breathers," he finished roughly, "we do not wish to kill."

"You could simply have left us where we were and let us drown," Spock pointed out.

A twinge of contempt was added to Domar's coldness.

"Indifference to the injured is merely another form of murder. A typical air-breather observation. You were brought here unconscious, barely alive. You were returned to a place near where you were found still unconscious, far more alive. Our obligation was discharged."

"It would seem that their own ancient records are as well preserved as ours," Cadmar put in. "They found us again anyway, to come among us as spies."

Again that shrill female voice cut the water. "You do not give them a chance to defend or explain themselves, Cadmar. Our law does allow that, even for unmentionable air-breathers who come among us."

"Rela is correct," said Domar, then turning back to Kirk and Spock. "You may speak . . . if you have the nerve."

"Look," Kirk began, ignoring Domar's invitation to fight, "you've apparently had some pretty bad experiences in the past with the last remnants of whatever branch of your race remained on the surface of this world. I can tell you with some assurance that you've no longer anything to fear from *that* quarter!

"As for ourselves, we come from another world entirely. Our only desire in returning to your city—which we found simply by following some of your farmers—was to . . ."

He did not get a chance to finish. The excitement his words had generated in the younger Tribunes finally spilled over.

"You do not live on the surface places?" Rela inquired wonderingly.

"Not of this world," Spock began, "we . . ."

The conversation was getting too complicated for Cadmar, at least. "Enough!" he cried, the violence of his comment bringing him out of his seat. "Clearly, this is a great lie. Another world, indeed! The situation is plain. The air-breathers are come again to wreak havoc among us."

"You are mistaken, sir," Spock objected quietly. "As Captain Kirk was about to say, our only purpose in returning here was to find a means of reversing the mutations you induced in us."

"That, at least, is impossible," Domar informed them brusquely. "There is nothing in the surgical records we retain that designates a method for reverse mutation."

Kirk slumped inwardly. That was it, then. He was doomed to spend the rest of his life drifting in a portable container. A curiosity, a freak for Federation scientists to ponder on and take periodic samples from.

Spock, undoubtedly, would handle it better than he. He wondered what it was going to be like to spend the rest of his life at the wrong end of a microscope.

The slight dot took on shape and form as Scott adjusted the telefocals. It resolved into a long, narrow creature with broad fins, a long thin tail, flapping wings and fishlike body. It skimmed low over the distant surface and he thought he could make out feathery gills on the back of the thing's neck.

Apparently an amphibious flier. Interesting. He wished Spock were here to see it and venture an opinion.

He wished Spock were here, period.

There was a buzz at his hip. He acknowledged the communicator call and McCoy's voice drifted up from the speaker.

"*Enterprise* to Mr. Scott."

Scott watched a moment longer as the flier folded leathery wings against its body and dove into the water. Then he turned his attention to the communicator.

"Scott here ... what is it, Doctor?"

"All departments have been proceeding with their own missions, as per Jim's orders, Scotty. We just got a bulletin from seismology. There's a major quake due in that area."

"How soon?"

"Meier can't be certain, but it's going to be a bad one. Complete topography shift."

"All right, he can't be exact ... I know those guys down there. What's their best estimate?"

A pause at the other end, and then McCoy's voice came back tense, worried. "Probably within four hours, Scotty. That's a conservative guess."

"And inside the captain and Mr. Spock's report-in time," he replied in alarm.

"Inside! Can't you contact them before that?"

"Kinna do it, Doctor. They've no communicators and ..." He stopped, thought a moment. "Wait ... there ought to be a trace signal from their translators. Those gadgets are small, but they use a lot of power. We can try like blue blazes, anyway. Scott out."

He flipped off, turned to the anxiously waiting Clayton. "Let's get out those other suits and the life-support belts, Lieutenant. Contact our other boats. We're goin' fishin'."

The green body suits were the closest thing to camouflage they had. But there was no way to disguise the glow from the belts. One by one the belts were activated and the little party dropped over the side.

Scott descended rapidly, braked to study the reading on the wrist guage he had donned along with the suit and belt. He turned slowly, finally stopped facing toward deeper water.

"Directional pickup indicates they're in that general direction, toward those dunes. Let's go." The little knot of crewmen started off in the indicated direction, shining like fireflies in the clear water.

Searching eyes roved over gorgeously colored underwater life, exotically shaped, remarkably shaded. Plant or animal or both, all were resolutely ignored. The party was hunting for more simply clad, more awkwardly built swimmers.

Two pairs of eyes studied them from behind a concealing dune of amber sand and rock. One pair belonged to one of the farmers Kirk and Spock had encountered earlier.

"More air-breathers," she reported to her companion. "We must inform the Tribunes." The other nodded and they streaked away, weaving in and out among the bemmies and beds of pseudo-kelp.

"The name of our starship, our above-the-air vessel," Kirk explained to the intent Tribunes, "is on the wreckage of our underwater craft. If you want proof, examine the remains."

"Yes," insisted Rela, "let us examine the wreckage before we pass judgment."

"To what end?" wondered Cheron tiredly. "The fact that their vessel has a name is no proof of extra-Argoan origin." Kirk was about to point out that they would find more conclusive evidence in the wreck when the discussion was interrupted by the breathless arrival of two females at the far end of the chamber. They rushed forward.

Kirk noted that no one objected to their entrance, no one sought to bar them from the room. This society had much to commend it, he reflected.

"Important news, High Tribune."

Domar made a curt gesture. "Speak."

"Several air-breathers have invaded the outskirts of

the cultivated areas. We saw them. They were moving toward the city. They glowed most strangely."

"That's only . . . ," Kirk began, but Doman drowned him out as he turned angrily to the Junior Tribunes. "Defensive screens, as the records speak of! Do you still believe these creatures come in peace?"

Some of Rela's self-righteous assurance faded, apparently drained by this unexpected information. "We do not know what to believe," she finally whispered unhappily.

Domar looked satisfied, turned his attention to the pair of guards who stood ready behind Kirk and Spock.

"Take these spies to the surface and leave them there. They wish to return to their element. So be it. Justice enough for our enemies . . . !"

IV

Kirk choked, gasped for breath. He got a half mouthful of water and gulped it gratefully.

Whether Domar, the other Tribunes, or the guards were responsible for the particular agony he and Spock were being subjected to he didn't know. But right now all he wished for was a smooth scaly neck under his fingers.

They had been taken to the spot where McCoy and Scott had found them and tied securely to the low-lying boulders there, just barely above the water line. Occasionally a wave would sweep over the rocks and give them a momentary respite from slow suffocation.

But the steady deprivation of air-rich water was making them weaker and weaker. At their present infrequent intake, they wouldn't last much longer. Nor was there any hope here of a life-giving incoming tide.

So weak were they that neither saw the slim form which swam nearby, staring at them sadly. Rela.

A glint of metal as the wave receded elsewhere caught her eye and she kicked toward it, her flippers propelling her rapidly through the water. Holding her breath, she poked her head and arms out of the water and examined the shards and scraps with a kind of resigned curiosity. Several of the pieces were bigger than she was and were almost intact. She noticed that one seemed to have some kind of writing etched into it. With her finger, she traced the cryptic indentations.

U.S.S. Enterprise ... the bumps meant nothing to her, of course.

Another section, caught high up on a rocky projection, caught her eye. She took a deeper breath, raised her head and stared. It seemed to be part of a dome ... a dome of some strange, transparent material. Judging from its curve, it must have enclosed a sub-

49

stantial area, though she couldn't get any good idea of its original size or shape. She clambered out onto the rocks, struggling clumsily.

Beneath the broken dome was a section of metal lined with interesting instruments. There were also several sealed cases which had broken loose from their catches and tumbled about within. One was jammed shut, but two of the others lay broken open, their contents scattered nearby.

She picked up the remains of what seemed to be a book—but the material was impossibly, incredibly fragile. Opening it carefully, she thumbed through it, her eyes growing wider and wider at each subsequent waterlogged revelation.

There were pictures of strange vessels, others of absurd underwater creatures she had never seen, and others—of air-dwellers! Such incredible monsters couldn't possibly exist ... on her world, she realized with a start.

And that meant ... she plunged into the water, swam furiously, perilously close to the sharp edges of the rocks. Taking another deep breath she scrambled up onto the flat boulder to which Kirk was bound, knelt over him.

"Conserve your strength," she bubbled, "I will free you ... somehow."

She tugged at the cords, trying to loosen the knots. She dug her flippers into a crack in the rocks and pulled with all her strength, gasping, straining, water running out her mouth and down her chin. No use.

While Kirk continued to gasp weakly she turned and plunged her head back under the surface for a long moment. Coming back up she said in that odd, gurgling voice, "The mesh is too strong!"

"Go," Kirk somehow managed to sputter, "toward the big island . . . assistance there, maybe . . . friends . . ."

Rela nodded, or at least that was the impression Kirk had. After giving both men long draughts of fresh water, she plunged back in and disappeared.

If, Kirk mused painfully, she decided not to come back . . .

Clayton looked over the side of the gig. A moment later, Scott, the lime-yellow aura of his life-support belt still glowing brightly, popped up. He reached up, clung to the side of the small craft.

"See anything?" asked Clayton. Scott shook his head dispiritedly.

"Still no sign of 'em. I wish we carried more underwater equipment. The captain and Mr. Spock are adapted for gettin' around in this environment. We just can't match 'em, tryin' to swim in a life-support aura.

"Besides which, the directional tracker isn't pickin' up their signal anymore. Lost it a while back and I'm damned if I know why . . . unless their translators are broken." He patted the one affixed to his own chest beneath the green bodysuit.

"The only signal I get now is from mine, and I'm not too sure *it* works. I thought I saw some big, man-shaped form watchin' us from one of the big kelp beds. I yelled at *it* and *it* disappeared."

"It might have been a fish," Clayton argued, "but I suppose it could have been one of our mysterious locals. I don't think it's the translator, sir, I . . ." He broke off, staring, as an alien shape broke the water only a couple of meters from the gig. His phaser came around automatically.

But it lowered at the same time they were given proof of the translator's efficacy.

"Follow me, quickly!" Rela implored. Without waiting for a reply, she turned and started off in the direction of the distant boulders.

"Wait a minute!" Scott shouted hurriedly, "who are . . . ?"

Rela whirled in the water, yelled back at them. "Follow me. Your friends need your help." She ducked her head and shot off again.

While Scott climbed into the gig, Clayton focused his telefocals on the distant, moving fin. "I've got her clearly, Mr. Scott. She's swimming just under the surface."

Scott nodded, switched off his life-support belt and moved to the controls of the gig. A second later the powerful side jets came to life and the compact vessel shot off in pursuit.

Kirk's chest felt like the rotten leather of an old bellows, and his hoarse rasping sounded like one. There were more pleasant ways to die, he thought, than suffocating to death. He sensed its nearness, and the first hallucinations confirmed it.

It started with the gurgling shout he dreamt he heard nearby. Vague forms seemed to move before his glazed eyes, almost human . . . angels, perhaps? It seemed that hands fumbled at his sides . . .

A warm coolness washed over him . . . a temperature incongruity? No . . . he drew in another breath, felt himself growing stronger, drew another and another.

His vision cleared with awesome abruptness, and he found himself staring into the non-angelic but no less welcome face of an anxious Scott. He sat up, looked around. Spock stared back at him across the sandy bottom.

Scott joined them, once again activating his yellow halo. Kirk seated himself on something soft and, he hoped, nonlethal.

"*Good* to see you, Scotty."

"Not as good as it is to see you, Captain." The look in the chief engineer's eyes embarrassed Kirk. He turned to Rela.

"Rela, this is my chief engineering officer, Mr. Scott. Tribune Rela is an Argoan-Aquan, as their name for themselves translates. Their city is a short distance away. I'm afraid Mr. Spock and I didn't make a very favorable impression on its rulers."

"We're obliged for your help," Scott said hurriedly, forcing gaze and curiosity away from the drifting Rela. "Captain, we've been trying to contact you for two hours. There's a severe quake due in this area soon. According to the seismology people, it will disrupt this entire region. That won't bother us, of course, but . . ."

The translators were good, not perfect. Some of the strange mouthings of the air-breathers came to Rela garbled and devoid of crucial nuances. But if some of the terminology was vague, the look Scotty gave her was enough to put his point across.

"There are many legends of such events," she told them. "When the great surface places sank into the sea. Much of the knowledge of the ancients was destroyed."

"I still do not understand," put in Spock, "how such a radical, complete racial mutation could take place in such a short time."

"You are right, Mr. Spock," Rela complimented him. "Evolution played no part in it. When the surface places began to sink, many air-breathers—my distant ancestors—were altered to breathe and live beneath the sea by surgery, as you were. Such surgery extended even to the . . ." it came out "genes."

"Thus, the change was made hereditary—for those who accepted the change. There were those who did not . . . hence my people's instinctive fear of you."

"Strange that the air-breathing remainder of your race should turn to useless violence," Kirk wondered, "considering their accomplishments."

"It seems as if those who remained on the surface didn't believe the continental subsidence would be this extensive," Spock theorized. "I would guess that somewhere, sometime, they lost the ability to change themselves into water-breathers. A few generations would serve to breed sufficient hatred and envy for those immune to the coming catastrophe."

"They hunted and killed among us," Rela recounted grimly. "We learned to hate anything that lives in the air. That is why it has always been forbidden to mutate back to such a state."

A startled glance passed between Kirk and Spock before the Captain commented excitedly to her, "Then reverse surgery *is* possible. Domar lied to us."

"Not wholly," Rela corrected. "There are stories of sealed places in the ancients' air-city where many records remain. It is rumored that . . ."

A dull rumbling echoed through the water around them. Sand was jolted upward, fish scurried frantically for the nearest cover, and Kirk and Spock found themselves bounced from their seats. The turbulence sent Scott and Rela tumbling slightly.

Sand continued to cascade in gritty falls from clumps of rock, clouding the water with drifting debris.

"Less than two hours," Scott warned them.

"How far are these ruins, Rela?" Kirk asked.

"Not far . . . in a direction away from the city."

Kirk already had his mind made up . . . but a second opinion was always good policy. "Mr. Spock?"

"We have no choice, Captain. If there is a chance for us, it lies there."

"But these are only stories," said Rela, alarmed at the reaction her information had produced. "In any case, I cannot take you there. It is against the Ordainments."

Kirk swam close to her. "It's vital, Rela. Not just for Mr. Spock and myself, but for the population of another world much like yours, threatened with similar disaster. Argo's ancient knowledge could help save them."

The Aquan hesitated, staring at the three aliens. If she chose to whirl and swim away it was doubtful that either Kirk or Spock could catch her. She made a sharp, enigmatic gesture.

"I will take you as far as the reef barrier." And before anyone could thank her, she had turned and started off at a right angle from the course back to the sunken city.

Kirk and Spock followed, having to push themselves to keep pace. It seemed as if they swam for hours, traveling over the endless amber-tinted plain, dodging coral heads and dunes.

Kirk noticed the way the fish thinned out as they moved on, and he wondered. Maybe it was something in the water, or maybe a lack of nutrients.

Rela seemed to be growing more and more nervous the further they swam, her eyes darting constantly in all directions. Looking for an aqueous poltergeist, he decided, would be a particularly difficult proposition.

It turned darker as they neared a barrier. A long, winding reef, much like the one he and Spock had encountered on their way to the Aquan city. Only this one was still living.

Rela came to a stop, gestured upward toward a

wide-mouthed hole in the rampart, lined with plants which jerked and swayed violently.

"The ruined city lies through there. Take care, the currents are strong."

"Aren't you coming with us?" Kirk asked.

"No," she replied emphatically, backing away, "I can go no further. I will wait for you with your friends."

She turned and, kicking powerfully, raced off into the distance. They would be wasting time and probably effort in trying to convince her to come with them. As one, both officers moved cautiously toward the gaping cavity.

Kirk soon felt a slight rippling of water over his body. It increased rapidly. Soon he was exerting all his strength just to stay in one place—but to no avail. The current had a firm grip on them and was pulling them inexorably into the cavern.

The interior of the cave soon showed blue sky overhead . . . it was another reef rift, not a tunnel. But the walls of this one were lined with jagged spikes of dead coral, twisted spines representing the combined toil of a billion tiny lives.

He fought the current, glad of his webbed hands and feet, as the suction pulled at them. Kicking furiously to stay level and at the same time avoid a reaching coral pike, he found himself wondering why Rela simply hadn't directed them to go over the top of the reef. The currents might be strong there, too, but could they be this violent?

Then it came to him. The reef probably stayed near the surface in most places, even breaking through. The idea of walking across the reef on one's flippers had probably never occurred to her.

Without warning, they were ejected from the reef. They came to a tumbling halt, still amid stone, but stone whose edges were not formed by a patient nature.

They were drifting in a giant's playpen of crumbling blocks and archways and unbalanced pylons—all jumbled together by some unimaginably violent cataclysm in Argo's past.

Down they drifted, past spires, turrets, towers, structures that resembled great temples, others that encircled a coral-encrusted marketplace. All alien, but still more familiar than the underwater city of the Aquans. This was a city made to live in the currents of wind, not water. A broad avenue curved away before them, lined with a crazy-quilt pattern of broken stone and paved here and there with the ever-present amber moss. Much of the sunken metropolis was overgrown with waving plant life. It stretched off to the horizon, dwarfing the city of the Aquans.

"Fascinating," Spock murmured. "Probably an entire portion of the continent sank within minutes and with minimal upheaval."

"Rela said the records repository would be a tall, triangular structure," Kirk reminded him. They started down the relatively clear avenue, eyeing dark crannies and long shadowed areas cautiously.

Of course, the Aquans' "Ordainments" were standard, superstitious taboos, but that didn't mean this skeleton city couldn't be home to some less ecclesiastical dangers.

As they moved deeper into the ruins they encountered buildings in a better state of preservation. Slanted towers rose around them, jagged cracks showing in their walls. But they still stood. How many more serious tremors their weakened foundations could stand Kirk could not tell.

The boulevard made a sharp turn to the right and they found themselves facing a broad plaza. At its far side stood a tall, pyramidal building. A deeply etched, gold-colored medallion was set into its top. The Argoan hieroglyphics were hardly eroded, testament to the knowledge of Rela's ancestors. The medallion shone brightly in the urban graveyard, catching the filtered sunlight.

At first it appeared the structure was blessed with a multitude of entrances. Ruined windows, broken doors—but all were blocked by internal collapse. They began to circle the building, checking each opening.

Then Spock spotted the large block that projected outward at the base of the building. Brushing aside sand, prying away encumbering shells, they uncovered a flat stone of a substance substantially different from the rest of the building. It looked more like alabaster than anything else, yet it was clearly artificial. Most important, there was a metallic emblem set into its front that matched the big disk at the building's apex.

Spock swam to the far side, dug webbed feet into the sand and shoved. For a moment nothing happened, then the block suddenly slid aside as though oiled.

Their lights revealed a clear passageway leading upward as far as the beams would reach ... and steps, honest steps.

A short swim brought them to the first of many interconnected chambers. Every other room was lined with drawers and cases of metal. After a little initial tugging, they came apart and broke open easily. Most of the cases were badly corroded, their contents long since destroyed.

Some, however, remained sealed, and these all had tiny plates of gleaming gold set into them. Each plate had a miniature bas-relief engraved in it, underlined by more of the indecipherable hieroglyphics. They went through a seemingly endless stream of sealed containers. In the sixth chamber Spock held one of the containers out and called to Kirk. Kirk dropped the one he was studying and swam over.

Alongside the expected rows of hieroglyphs was cut the form of an upright human figure, split down the middle. One side of the torso was normal. The other resembled, more than anything else, the body of a fish.

"I do not think the meaning could be more clear, Captain." Spock gestured at the open case behind him. "There are three others set with the same engraving, a fourth with something rather nauseating. I only hope they hold medical records and not the reproduced work of some long-dead Argoan surrealist."

The men swam rapidly now, tracing their path back out of the temple or museum or hospital or whatever it had been, back toward the edge of the city.

A long, curved pillar marked the end of the avenue, a roadblock to fleeing inhabitants during the age-old disaster, but not to swimmers. The obstruction lay across the road from still upright cousins, supporters of a dark mausoleum to their right.

Spock started upward then halted in mid-stroke. Kirk pulled up just as sharply behind him. He had noticed the movement in the fallen column, too.

Another column joined the first, fluttering. A huge form rose into view from behind the partly ruined structure. They weren't stone, those columns; and Kirk frantically damned himself for not recognizing the first.

They were the arms of a creature they had met before, a creature capable of blind fury and incredible strength. If anything, this snake-squid was even bigger than the one that had destroyed the shuttle.

They turned and swam furiously back up the avenue. The snake-squid started to follow, its roars rattling Kirk's water-filled ears. Evidently they had stumbled across one that had been half asleep, or they would both have been fish-fodder already.

He looked back over his shoulder. The muscles in his legs were starting to knot up under the unaccustomed demand. The monster was still well behind them, but closing ground fast. It still wasn't fully awake.

Another roar shook him—literally. A deeper, grinding scream that sent him tumbling head over heels. Walls and towers came crumbling down around them as the quake tortured the old buildings. Kirk held onto his two cylinders for dear life.

One gigantic block of cut stone struck their pursuer near the skull. It paused, drifted motionless in the water for a moment, stunned. Then it suddenly turned—all thoughts of tiny prey forgotten now—and rocketed away.

For long minutes they lay in the protective shadow of the hospital-temple, ready to dart back into the entranceway at the first sign of a probing tentacle.

"A most interesting creature," Spock commented. "Instinctively aggressive and blessed with remarkable offensive equipment. It would be interesting to . . ."

Kirk managed a grin, held up the pair of cylinders he was carrying. "If these don't contain the necessary medical information, we may have an ample number of years to study it first hand."

No further tremors troubled them as they left the city this time, nor did they encounter the snake-squid or any other predator.

Returning through the hole in the reef was pretty much out of the question. Possibly one of Rela's people could have bucked the powerful current, but Kirk didn't think his legs could manage it. Fortunately, they were able to confirm an earlier supposition.

Swimming upward, they discovered that the reef did indeed break the surface in numerous places. By walking carefully and taking deep breaths at the multitude of pools that pockmarked the top, they were able to cross it on foot. Even so, Kirk was relieved when they finally reached the far side and were able to descend once again. He could understand why the Aquans were reluctant to consider such an idea.

One sealed cylinder proved a complete dead end, but the others contained between them the complete details of the air-to-water mutation procedure, as well as water-to-air. There was also a great amount of additional information which kept much of the *Enterprise*'s scientific staff drooling over the shoulders of the linguists. As each new revelation or bit of ancient theory was translated, a small covy of men and women would bear away their booty for intensive study with all the enthusiasm of a bunch of Goths at the sack of Rome.

Kirk pressed up against the glass of the water room and stared out at McCoy. Two-way pickups brought the soft click-click of the computer annex through to him as the doctor ran through the relevant material a final time.

McCoy was hoping to find a substitute for the prescribed methodology. Failing that, he had searched for a substitute for one particular compound. No use. The formula specified by the ancient Argoans was inflexible.

Turning, he spoke into the pickup. "If the translations are all correct, Jim, the mutations are brought about by a timed series of injections. To return your

circulatory and respiratory systems to normal, supposedly all we have to do is provide you with sufficient
dosages at properly spaced intervals."

Kirk waited. When McCoy didn't continue, he ventured, "Only . . . there's a problem."

"Yes. I can duplicate most of the required chemicals
in the lab . . . except for a derivative from a local
venom. Weirdest arrangement of proteins you ever saw.
No way I can synthesize it."

"All right," Kirk replied calmly, "where do we get
it?"

"It's a good thing the chemical text was accompanied
by diagrams . . . and pictures. Not surprisingly, the
venom is produced by the poison glands of a large local
meat-eater. Judging by both the visual and written material, its not as rare as the Argoans wished it was."

He touched another switch, punched out a combination on a keyboard in the annex. There was a hum and
a sheet of printed plastic popped out of a slot. McCoy
took it, walked over to the glass and pressed the sheet
up against it.

Kirk and Spock studied the carefully reproduced
drawing made by some long-dead Argoan biologist.
They ignored the translated text because they didn't
need it. The creature sported a snakelike body, a circu-
lar, toothed gullet, and four enormous tentacles.

McCoy pulled the sketch away. "I don't know where
you're going to find one, or how you're going to capture it. The venom must be taken while the creature is
alive and active. A phaser stun would numb the poi-
son-injection mechanism. Dissection is out, too, because
death causes the venom to lose its potency immediately.
It's got to be gathered while the creature is alive and
kicking."

"Don't worry about us finding one, Bones," Kirk assured him. "As for handling a live one, we've already
had plenty of experience in how not to . . ."

Rela had arranged a clandestine meeting on the outskirts of the cultivated areas. The two other young
Tribunes, Nefrel and Lemas, listened attentively to

Kirk's description of the impending quake. Their looks turned to alarm when he began to detail the request.

"We need your help to capture one of the snake-squids ... alive," he told them, "snake-squid" coming out as a series of unpronounceable gurglings. "We can't do it ourselves—the only craft we possess for performing such tasks here was destroyed by one of the creatures."

The three young Aquans exchanged uneasy glances. "Rela was observed leading you toward the Forbidden Zone," Nefrel explained. "Domar has warned us that if we break the Ordainments again we risk being exiled to the open seas."

"We cannot reverse the mutations you induced in us without the serum the captain has told you about," Spock said firmly, "and we cannot make that serum without the snake-squid's venom."

"But the Ordainments," Nefrel persisted, "also state that capturing one is forbidden."

"See how all is cleverly tied together!" Lemas exclaimed. "It is forbidden to capture a *cpheryhm-aj* because its poison is needed to reverse the sea-change. Tell me, Nefrel, will the Ordainments protect us from the upheaving of the sea-floor? These travelers say their science can help us, but we must help them first. That is just."

Kirk didn't bother to correct Lemas. They would aid the Aquans as best they could, no matter what.

"We must break the Ordainments, Nefrel," insisted Rela, "even if Captain Kirk could not aid us."

The reluctant Tribune finally acquiesced, whereupon the five left the meeting place and started back toward the sunken city of the ancients.

"We do not need to return to *Llach-sse*," Lemas told him. "We can obtain what we need from the outlying storehouses."

Kirk's confidence suffered an unexpected letdown when he saw that the three Aquans intended to use to capture one of the huge carnivores. It was a net ... uncomplicated, with no secret devices of a subtle undersea science concealed in it.

Of course, he and Spock had been unable, despite

their most violent efforts, to so much as loosen a strand
of the net that had been used to capture them. Maybe
the material was far stronger than he had suspected. He
eyed the thin webbing and hoped so.

This was no time for criticism of the Aquans' efforts—he had to hope they knew what they were doing.

The next step took a great deal of persuasion on
Kirk and Spock's part. Lemas and Nefrel in particular
refused to believe one could simply walk over the forbidden reef and avoid the treacherous, current-torn
crevice.

But exhilaration replaced fear when they finally
completed the crossing, without a single injury or moment of panic.

Trying to stay out of sight as much as possible, they
circled the city and approached the entrance from behind, from the region of the hospital-temple. Kirk
hoped they would be able to find the large *cypheryhm-
aj* that had ambushed them before.

Rela was swimming well in advance of the rest of
the party. Suddenly, she put up a hand in a trans-cul-
tural gesture, and they moved up quietly alongside her.

When Kirk and Spock had stumbled across the
snake-squid it had been dazed and drowsy, half asleep.
Now it appeared fully quiescent, perhaps sleeping off
the blow it had absorbed from the falling stone. It lay
motionless on the sand, coiled in among a cluster of
huge boulders.

Kirk knew how deceptive that peaceful scene was.
At any moment, any suspicious sound, the monster
might awaken and make a quick meal of them all. That
another timely quake would be in the offing was highly
unlikely.

Carefully the three Aquans unrolled their weighted
net. Lemas and Nefrel unfurled it while Rela took care
to keep it parallel to the bottom and untangled.

At a mutual sign, they started swimming smooth and
fast for the snake-squid.

Either they reached a crucial point or someone lost
his nerve, because both Lemas and Nefrel suddenly
stopped moving forward. Rela let go of the back end of
the net. Inertia and weight kept the net moving forward

and curving slightly downward. All three Aquans retreated toward the crumbled wall they had left . . . and waited, and watched.

Falling in a gentle arc, the net kept its shape as it neared the bottom, began to settle softly over the snake-squid. The beast quivered slightly when the first strands touched it; but when the body of the net made contact, the *cpheryhm-aj* erupted.

While Kirk and Spock watched anxiously, unable to intervene for fear of getting in someone's way at a critical moment, the three Aquans shot downward.

The more the monster struggled, the tighter the mesh was drawn. Both officers admired the design of the net, which they now saw was equipped with an intricate series of cross-pulls and cords that tightened around any prey.

And Kirk's hopeful analysis of the netting was proven correct . . . not a strand parted, not a square broke.

Judging from the urgency in Rela's voice as she yelled to them to hurry, its invincibility was finite, however. Both officers moved rapidly downward, hurriedly readying the makeshift container-collectors McCoy had designed, flexible pouches from each of which protruded a long suction tube with a wide mouth.

The snake snake-squid had a better view of the officers than it did of the dodging, darting Aquans. Tentacles and teeth strained for the two maddeningly near shapes. Reflex reaction sent a jet of dark fluid toward both men.

Kirk edged the mouth of a suction tube into the slowly dispersing cloud, touched a control on the side of the tube. He moved the flexible gathering mouth from side to side. McCoy had warned them that they needed as much venom as they could obtain.

Dark poison dissipated around the captain. The Aquans had assured him the poison was harmless unless injected. He kept that resolutely in mind as he directed the tube toward a darker patch, missed it when a sudden current sent him tumbling.

Rubble showered down from surrounding towers. Much of the already battered structure they'd hidden behind came down. Some of the venom already collected drifted from the open mouth of the suction tube and Kirk hurriedly closed it off. A series of violent after-shocks made things more difficult. Rela was alongside him unexpectedly, watching the procedure worriedly. She directed his attention downward.

While the admirable material of the net had proven equal to the explosive spasms of the snake-squid, it had fallen victim to some of the toppling stone. Rocks and carved pillars had driven the pinioned carnivore into a frenzy. They had also abraded sections of the net to the point where the monster was able to break them.

It was still trapped, still bound awkwardly ... but it had discovered the weakened portions and was tearing at them with mindless malevolence.

"We must leave now, quickly," Rela insisted. She turned, started for the top of the reef where they would be safe.

Kirk examined a gauge set in the side of the tube, called after her. "We need more venom."

"There is no time!" she shouted back. "There ..."

A thunderous, echoing moan drowned out her last words. Two of the muscular tentacles and part of the upper body of the snake-squid were already free of the netting. Another minute or two and the creature would free the rest of its thick torso. They couldn't hope to outswim the maddened beast.

Cursing silently, Kirk raced off in pursuit of the retreating Aquans. Spock risked a reaching tentacle for one last inhalation of poison before following.

V

Kirk had tried floating on his head, swimming off the walls, counting rocks—in general, doing everything imaginable to dampen his impatience while McCoy ran a final series of checks on the mildly toxic chemical.

So many things could go wrong if even a small portion of the ancient formulae was wrong, out of date, inaccurately set down. And there was no Aquan physician present to look for signs of failure.

Kirk studied McCoy and Nurse Chapel as they moved slowly in their underwater gear—too much precision was required now for life-support belts.

With Chapel's aid, McCoy was locking a small bottle of fluid into a spray-contact hypo. Now, if only Spock's metabolism and his would adapt to Argoan medical procedure as readily as did Bones' equipment.

McCoy's voice, distorted by the broadcast apparatus and the intervening water, broke the nervous silence.

"We've set this up as best we can, Jim. Only a small section of the relevant records was missing. I don't think—I *hope*—it isn't critical."

"But I thought you said . . . ," Kirk began.

McCoy made calming motions. "Oh, I'm sure about the composition of the serum, Jim, that portion of the records is intact and plenty scientific. The section that's missing . . ." He shook his head.

"Something to do with the dosage per unit of body weight. I've had to approximate without the complete charts. We might never turn them up." He motioned the two men toward the bedlike slabs that would serve as a resting place.

"The experiments I ran on local fish-life show that if the serum dosage is too strong, it causes an over-mutation which then can't be reversed by any means. Inject

65

too little and there can be violent side effects. The stuff is tricky, and too potent for my liking.

"I'd like to conduct further experiments, but we . . ."

"Haven't got enough venom," Spock finished for him.

"Not only that, but the potency of what you brought back fades rapidly. The composite serum has to be used right away. If you could obtain some more . . ." He stared at Kirk, but the captain made a negative gesture.

"We've already drawn on our credit with Rela and her friends to the point of exhaustion, Bones. I'm not sure we could convince them to repeat the hunt. I'm not sure I want to . . . we might not be so lucky a second time." McCoy sighed, resigned.

"Then I'll have to make do. I've decreased the maximum allowable dosage by one quarter—that should be proper for your systems, Vulcan as well as human."

Kirk nodded. "All right. How many infusions?"

"Two small, one large."

"Let's get started."

Both officers assumed reclining positions on the slabs, head higher than feet. McCoy checked a gauge on the side of the hypo, made a last adjustment. If he had miscalculated half a cubic centimeter either way, the damage to their bodies could be irreversible.

McCoy pressed the hypo's nozzle to Kirk's upper arm, then stepped back and studied his wrist chronometer intently. Several minutes slid by before the first change appeared.

Kirk's skin was changing, the pigmentation darkening slightly. First it deepened to a rich golden hue, then to a familiar amber. The captain's lids drooped low, lower, finally closed tightly.

Abruptly, the amber color drained like bourbon from a broken bottle, leaving Kirk a pale, nearly albino white. They all studied him anxiously, but he showed no signs of movement. McCoy frowned uneasily and hurried to exchange the hypo for a pre-keyed tricorder.

He passed it carefully over Kirk's limp form, muttering to himself all the while. "Pulse fading . . . all internal functions slowed . . . heartbeat weakened . . ."

"Andrenalin . . . aldrazine?" ventured Chapel. McCoy shook his head, pulled the 'corder away.

"There's enough in his system now that doesn't belong there. Give the serum another couple of minutes."

Sure enough, normal color began to tint Kirk's face, returning with the same suddenness it had departed. He stirred slightly on the makeshift pallet.

Chapel let out a bubbling sigh of relief. Spock remained expressionless as usual, but McCoy noticed how an unnatural tenseness had suddenly left the first officer's muscles.

Again he made a pass with the tiny machine. "Pulse and heart normal, other shifts within acceptable parameters . . . good. Nurse?"

Chapel handed him the second of the three bottles and he exchanged it for the first, reset the dial on the side of the hypo. This time he pressed it over the Captain's chest, just below the left lung, held it there a second, then moved it to the right side and repeated the injection.

Kirk's body reacted instantly this time, jerking spasmodically on the slab like a puppet with snipped strings. Before McCoy could have countered with another injection of any kind, Kirk collapsed. Once more the amber hue flooded his face. Once again McCoy used the compact 'corder.

"Something's really given his system a kick—his metabolism's a good ten times normal speed."

"Doctor," Spock interrupted, "his hands."

McCoy's gaze moved down the unconscious form. The thin webbing which had formed between the fingers was dissolving like so much gelatin, the faint scaling beginning to smooth out. His stare went lower and he saw that the same process was at work on the feet.

McCoy checked his watch, made yet another pass with the instrument.

"Metabolism normal—and everything else!" He couldn't keep the optimism from his voice, didn't want to. "Indication of physiological alteration in the lungs . . . he's beginning a complete reversal. Nurse . . ."

Chapel handed him the final bottle. Carefully

McCoy locked the vial in place beneath the pistol-like hypo.

"This is the final dose," he said, to no one in particular. "The major infusion. Roll him over please, Christine."

Chapel slowly turned Kirk on his stomach . . . easy enough in the water. McCoy recalled the translated instructions, prayed that the ancient recorder was precise in his technique and made the last injection as it had been described.

He pulled the hypo away, nodded to her. She turned Kirk over on his back again, let him relax. Nothing happened. McCoy was about to program a minute secondary dose when Kirk suddenly doubled up in agony, his legs threshing wildly and an expression of pure pain invading his face.

The pitiful moans of a man having nightmares filled the water around them. Scales erupted like scars on his face and the backs of his hands.

Twitching with uncontrollable violence, he spun from the pallet and onto the sand. So powerful were the jerks and kicks that McCoy and Spock were unable to get a grip on him.

Finally the explosion quieted and Kirk came to rest motionless and face down on the sand. The back of the skin-tight green bodysuit started to bulge slightly, showing an eruption of dorsal fin. Chapel didn't scream—she'd seen too many mistakes of nature in McCoy's lab to be terrified by another—but her eyes widened in horror. Spock, uncharacteristically, looked helpless.

"Too strong . . . the serum was too strong!" McCoy groaned. The spasms struck again and once more Kirk was thrashing water. The amber color deepened even further and revealed a faint yellowish overlay.

But this time, as he twisted in the sand, the scales that had formed momentarily on his face and hands began to fade, the bulge on his back disappeared and was reabsorbed.

The kicking and tumbling slowed, stopped. As he lay still on the bottom the yellow tinge vanished from his skin, followed soon thereafter by the amber. McCoy drifted over to the limp form. Again the tiny tricorder did its work.

When McCoy looked up again there was a note of satisfaction in his voice. "He's starting to breathe steadily again. Quick, we must get him out of the tank."

Together, the three of them wrestled the motionless body into the airlock. Spock remained inside. While McCoy supported Kirk, Chapel manipulated the controls. Both watched Kirk's face nervously as the drains in the floor rapidly sucked the water from the lock.

Kirk started to choke, flailing at the water with both arms. McCoy didn't wait for the water to leave completely. Instead, he slammed a palm down on the red button on the console labeled *Emergency Cycle*.

They nearly fell as a gush of water half-carried them from the airlock. Together they laid the captain on the floor. He stopped kicking almost immediately, coughed a couple of times, water dribbling from one side of his mouth.

Then he rolled over, still wheezing, but with less force now. The coughing finally died and then he was breathing deeply again—and for the first time in a long while, normally.

"Easy, Jim, how do you feel?"

Kirk continued to take long draughts of air, eyed McCoy as if the doctor were a little unbalanced. "Tired, a bit dizzy . . . otherwise fine."

Chapel reappeared with a large thermal blanket. She draped it around Kirk's shoulders as he got to his feet.

"Better make dry clothes your first priority, Jim," McCoy advised him. "Along with the metamorphosis of your respiratory and circulatory systems, there've been some extensive changes in your epidermal layers. I half anticipated them, from what the old records said. But so help me, I didn't think they'd come color-coded!" He grinned. "After what you've just been through, it would be damned silly for you to catch a cold."

Kirk nodded, then McCoy turned his attention to the water room's remaining occupant. "You're turn next, Spock, if after watching, you still want to go through with it."

Spock's gaze remained on Kirk. Only when the captain finally gave him an "everything's okay" smile did he reply, "I await the procedure with a modicum of impatience, Doctor." That was just Spock's way of saying the waiting was driving him up the walls.

Kirk sat down in the command chair ... slowly, enjoying the use of his legs for something other than horizontal locomotion, luxuriating in the chair's dryness more than anything else.

He looked left, to where Spock and Scott were explaining the various functions of the bridge's instrumentation to the goggling Domar and Rela.

Both Tribunes wore body suits and transparent, water-filled masks. Their tanks rested on the back of the wheelchairs that Scott's people had improvised.

It had taken all Scott's persuasive powers to convince even the adventurous Rela that the strange attire would keep them alive and healthy out of the water. But it was Domar who had agreed to the trial visit to the *Enterprise* first.

The qualities which had made him High Tribune dictated that he not appear craven before mere air-breathers, nor allow a Junior Tribune to seem the braver. Actually, he resented the powered chairs more than the water-suits. But while his legs were immensely powerful, they would tire rapidly under the steady pull of gravity in a waterless environment—and his flippers were not designed for walking.

So it was necessary for him and Rela to tour the *Enterprise* from the self-contained chairs. In the shadow of many wonders, however, he rapidly lost all sense of indignity.

Just now he was staring at a large rectangle of light in the middle of which a multicolored globe hung poised against speckled blackness. The air-breather next to him, the one called Scott, had assured him that what he was looking at was his own world—all of it.

Normally, he would not even have deigned to laugh at the air-breather. But he had seen enough of this magical vessel to convince him that anything might be true. Why, he was still trying to recover from the claim that there was neither water nor air outside this ship!

The one called Kirk, Tribune-equal, was gesturing at the screen. From his chest, a small machine carried mechanical-sounding words to the High Tribune, who struggled to fathom their meaning and glimpsed it dimly. Many of the air-breather's words translated poorly, while others, he was afraid, would remain forever only noises to him.

"Careful placement of a few large photon torpedoes, combined with a selective bombardment of fault areas with phaser beams, should shift the epicenter of the quake sufficiently northward for your city to survive with minimal damage," Kirk was saying.

"That's what the theory claims, anyway. It's a technique we planned to try. Now we have something more than an abstract reason to attempt it for. We think it has an excellent chance of working."

"Ninety-four point seven percent," Spock qualified.

Comprehension of what these people were about to try was enough to finally overcome Domar's aloofness.

"I did not believe such knowledge existed." For the first time he permitted himself an open stare of amazement, taking in the entire sweep of the bridge.

"It is incredible ... all of this."

"Approximately three minutes to the first significant fault shift, Captain." Kirk glanced back to the engineering station.

"Thank you, Mr. Scott. Mr. Spock, confirm coordinates for torpedo strike to effect re-alignment of epicenter."

Spock bent over his hooded viewer. "Confirmed, sir." He looked up. "The results should prove most interesting. To my knowledge, this will be the first time in Federation history that a starship's offensive armament has been deployed according to the instructions of the geology section."

Kirk turned his attention to the helm-navigation console. "Mr. Arex, Mr. Sulu, I know that the coordinates and firepower required has all been precalculated and preprogramed. Hold yourselves in readiness, however, for any last minute adjustments. They have a way of cropping up at the most awkward times."

"Aye, sir" ... "Aye, Captain," came the dual acknowledgment.

Kirk nodded once. "Fire torpedoes, first phasers."

Both men initiated the sequence of computer-directed firepower that would alter the internal heavings of a planet.

Far to the north of the submerged Aquan city, several super-fast objects dropped through the amber-hued atmosphere and vanished beneath the surface of the roiling sea. So fast did they travel that there was no towering fountain of water, no great splash where they entered.

Nor was there any sound. But far, far below the waves the multiple detonations of the precisely spaced photon torpedoes created a shock wave felt for hundreds of kilometers around.

Seconds later, while the deep-water creatures and bottom ooze were still settling back into ages-old quiescence, twin beams of light brighter than a sun lit the underwater abyssal plain with a radiance that illumined simple-minded crawlers for the first and last time of their primitive lives.

"Report, Mr. Spock."

"Too early yet to tell, Captain," Spock declared without looking up from the viewer. "Another minute or so before the major shift is due."

Domar still did not entirely comprehend what was taking place around him. Nor did he understand the process by which certain things were being altered. He knew only that these strange people, these air-breathers from (was it possible?) another world, were presently engaged in some obscure activity that would decide one way or another the fate of his beloved city.

Domar did not for a moment think that whatever the outcome of that activity he, at least, was safe from impending destruction. He *was* aware that the motives of these beings were not wholly altruistic. From what he had been told they had a world of their own much like his on which some day in the future a similar crisis was likely to occur. If proven successful, the methods now being employed to save his people would someday be utilized to save their own.

He mentioned nothing of this. For one thing, everyone in this chamber of miracles was silent and expectant now, in a way that suggested they were hardly indifferent to the outcome of their efforts. For another, voicing his dark suspicions would have been undiplomatic.

Spock's voice, when he finally elected to break the silence, was no higher, no louder, no more expressively modulated than ever. But it resounded on the tense bridge like the brass section of an orchestra.

"Sensors indicate," he announced, "that the epicenter of the just-concluded quake was in the north polar seas, Captain . . . a totally uninhabited area, according to Domar's people."

The interpretation was a bit much for even the usually omnipotent translators to manage. Domar looked at once relieved and confused.

"This means, then, that my people are safe?"

"That's right, Tribune," Kirk said happily, turning from the screen to face him. "It doesn't mean, though, that your city won't be subject to such dangers in the future. We can't make the ground around your city more stable. All we can do is *bleed* the instability to a region where no one will be endangered."

"What the captain is saying, Tribune Domar," Spock elucidated, "is that the technique we have used is effective, if not constructive."

"When can we beam down, Spock?"

"The section of sub-continent on which the Aquan city is built has been subjected to a considerable if not violent realignment of the substrata, Captain. This will stabilize fully within a few hours . . ."

"Where would you like to be set down, sir?"

Kirk took up his position in the transporter alcove, next to Spock. Domar and Rela sat in their chairs by the transporter console, looked on in fascination. They had expressed a desire to see the process by which they'd been brought aboard and would beam down later.

He eyed Chief Kyle thoughtfully. "You have the

coordinates of the spot where Dr. McCoy and Chief Scott first found us after we'd been changed?"

Kyle punched appropriate switches, checked a readout and nodded.

"I think that will do, Chief."

"All right, sir. Energizing."

"Perhaps someday, Mr. Spock," Kirk began, as he felt the familiar disorienting caress of the transporter, "they'll take this danged whine out of the transporter mechanism."

Spock didn't have time to reply.

Just before a person winked out for elsewhere the whine rose to an unbearable pitch and for a split second he felt like his teeth were coming apart. Not that they weren't, of course, but the sensation of dental disintegration was distressingly convincing.

The ocean of Argo was as softly amber and calm as Kirk remembered it, with wave-crests the hue of cream chiffon. The memory of the transporter computer was also accurate. They were standing on a pile of jumbled rocks and dead coral, just slightly above sea-level. But something was wrong, something had changed.

The shallow pool where Scott and McCoy had discovered their water-breathing forms lay just below and to their left, all right . . . but now it was only a low sand-filled depression scooped out of the rocks. And the little island seemed much increased in area. He looked to the other side, saw jagged bits of metal and plastic. The remains of the long-ruined underwater shuttle.

No, this was their proper pile of stone . . . only it had been raised high above the water. Spock noticed Kirk's uncertainty, explained.

"Sensors indicated considerable subsidence of the sea bottom near the quake's epicenter, Captain. It was apparently accompanied by a corresponding rise of the ocean bed in this area."

He pointed behind them.

The basalt fortress which had dominated their attention when they had first set down on Argo now towered even further into the azure sky. The shift here hadn't been unduly violent, for the wreaths of moss drooped undisturbed from unbroken crags and spires. But there was clear evidence of change nonetheless. Instead of dropping sheer into crashing waves, the island was now ringed by a broad beach of dark sand, until recently part of the bottom.

Kirk sniffed, wrinkled his nose and found ample olfactory hints of change, too. Fish and other ocean dwellers, too slow or stupid to flee the slow rise, had been trapped by the receding waters in small pools, now evaporated. Decay had set in with a vengeance and generated a miasma in sharp contrast to the visual splendor of the scene.

But the most spectacular sight of all lay hidden from view until they rounded the crest of the island. It took Kirk only seconds to place that graveyard of toppled towers, imploded domes, tumbled rocks and alabaster walls and foundation stones. Despite the upheaval, the sunken city of the Aquans' air-breathing ancestors had risen once more into the light fairly intact. Now it lay exposed and naked, drying in the bright sun of midday like some massive pressed flower.

"Argo appears to have a new city, Captain," Spock observed, "or rather, one reborn."

"Well put, Mr. Spock," a new voice agreed. They turned.

Domar spoke as he and Rela struggled from the water, masks and tanks still in place. They moved better on the soft sand than they had on the *Enterprise*, but Kirk and Spock walked politely down to meet them at water's edge, nonetheless.

"We did not entirely escape the effects of the quake," Rela informed them, indicating that she and Domar had beamed down to the city, "but our people survived with minimal damage—and less injury—thanks to your help. If we had remained near what you call the epicenter, we surely would have been destroyed."

"We owe you and your companions much gratitude, Captain Kirk," Domar said gravely. There was an odd emphasis on the word "gratitude," as if the translator had been unable to reflect the Aquan's meaning exactly and had selected only the closest analog.

"Is there nothing we can do for you?"

"The ability to transform us into water-breathers," Kirk explained, "is something on which our scientists have labored for many hundreds of years, with only the most limited success. If we might have permission to make copies of those and other medical records of your ancestors . . . ?"

"All will be placed at your disposal, Captain Kirk." assured Domar. "What we have left, of life as well as knowledge, you have given us. It is yours by right."

Such adulatory obeisance made Kirk acutely uncomfortable. There were many times when Spock's directness was welcome. Now he relieved Kirk by changing the subject.

"The technique of utilizing starship firepower to alter stress patterns in fault systems has been proven effective. By permitting us to do this you have enabled us to test a method which will mean much to threatened Federation worlds with similar problems."

Domar made the Aquan equivalent of a smile. "It takes a consummate diplomat to make salvation come out like an apology, Mr. Spock."

"So bright, so warm it is here!" Rela purred, stretching lazily. "I will be glad when the surface places can be inhabited."

"It will have to be done slowly, carefully," Kirk admonished her. "You'll need more than the ability to breathe air. There's the problem of your skin, for example."

"What's wrong with my skin?"

"As it stands, nothing," Kirk dead-panned. "But it's adapted to a perpetually moist environment. It will dry out, crack, and blister unless given some form of protection . . . such as the body suit you're currently wearing."

He frowned abruptly.

"What do you mean, 'inhabited?' "

Domar gestured toward the risen city of the ancients. "The young among us have decided to rebuild the great shelters of our forebears."

"Only the young?" Kirk queried. Domar sounded apologetic.

"Mature Aquans cannot adjust to the thought of becoming air-breathers. There are no formulas in the old records for altering one's outlook on such things. So most of us will remain in the world we know. Air-life is for the pioneers among us."

"Don't lose contact with each other like your ancestors did, in case of another continental adjustment."

"We will pass ordainments to forbid this."

"And this time we won't ignore them," Rela finished impishly.

"It is always the psychological and not physiological differences that are the real dangers," Spock pointed out. He nodded at Kirk. "The history of Captain Kirk's own world is especially revealing in this respect."

Rela stared at Kirk in surprise. "You have water-breathers on your home world too, Captain?"

"No." The young Tribune looked disappointed. "Mr. Spock is referring to the fact that in my people's past, great conflicts took place which supposedly had their root causes in small physical differences, but which were actually centered in the mind. Small minds seize upon such differences to exploit their own mental deficiencies . . . apparently a universal trait."

A faint fog began to form in front of his eyes, and he saw that a familiar glow was beginning to distort his view of Spock.

"What happened to the others?" Rela asked quickly. "Were they exterminated?"

"Others?" Kirk's mind reaced. "Oh, you mean the ones who were different? As I said, the bodily differences meant nothing. In the end, the ones with the mental imbalances found themselves pitied into extinction."

"I don't understand, Captain Kirk," came the final confused words of the Aquan, of Rela, the water-sprite.

A mild stab of nausea shook him as his perception of the universe went blotto. "Neither did they," he finished.

"I beg your pardon, sir?" said a puzzled Chief Kyle. Kirk blinked. They were back on board the *Enterprise*. "Did you say something about extinction, sir?"

Kirk noticed Spock was watching him with mild interest. "No, Mr. Kyle . . . nothing at all. *Execution* . . .

I was complimenting you on the execution of your duties."

"Thank you, sir," Kyle replied uncertainly.

Kirk stepped out of the transporter alcove, with Spock following right behind. Spock noticed the smile spreading slowly over the Captain's face.

"You find something amusing, Captain?"

"The timing of certain demands made by the human body, Spock."

"Now *that* is a subject for considerable amusement," Spock agreed drily. "What particular aberration of your unfortunate self strikes you as humorous at the moment?"

"The fact, Spock, that, after all I've gone through this past week, immediately upon leaving Argo I can find myself experiencing the desire I currently do."

"Which is?" his first officer prompted.

Kirk's smile twisted slightly. "I'm thirsty." Spock continued to stare at him and Kirk stopped, his smile fading. "Well, what's the matter, Spock? You may not find it funny, but . . ."

"It's not that, Captain, the humorous coefficients of the elemental coincidence are decidedly scrutable. I merely am appalled at my lack of basic knowledge where the human body is concerned."

"What do you mean?" Kirk eyed him unsurely.

"I had not known that a case of aggravated thirst . . ."

"It isn't aggravated," Kirk protested, but Spock ignored and went on.

". . . could produce such startling changes in pigmentation. Or perhaps it has nothing to do with thirst at all, but is an after-reaction to our retransformation back to normal."

"Spock, what the hell are you talking about?"

"You will see more clearly in a mirror, Captain. No," he put up a hand to forestall the coming words, "I am not talking in riddles, Captain. You know me better than that. But your coloration most definitely is not normal. How do you feel?"

"Thirsty, as I said . . . and a little tired. Normal

enough, under the circumstances." His voice turned slightly irritable. "I feel perfectly fine, Spock ... I don't know what you mean. 'Coloration' again! It's nothing at all, nothing at all ..."

PART II

THE
PIRATES
OF
ORION

(Adapted from a script by Howard Weinstein)

VI

"Captain's log, stardate 5527.3," Kirk declaimed into the armchair pickup as he surveyed the bridge. "My 'nothing at all' turned out to be the first symptoms of choriocytosis.

"Despite an initial outbreak during which several members of the crew apparently contracted the disease simultaneously, it appears to be under control now. Dr. McCoy insists it's no longer even as dangerous as pneumonia, and we have experienced no significant drop in performance. Therefore I foresee no difficulties in completing our newly assigned mission—representing the Federation at the dedication ceremonies for the new interspecies Academy of Science on Deneb Five." He clicked off the log, looked to his left.

"Status, Mr. Spock?"

"All systems operating at prime efficiency, Captain. We are on course and on schedule. I anticipate no deviations from the norm."

Kirk leaned back in the command chair and mused on the arduous duty they would be subjected to upon making landfall on Deneb Five. They would be forced to cope with an endless round of parties, gourmet dinners, the brilliant conversation of new acquaintances and the warm chatter of old ones. Yet, after what they had been through these past several months, he somehow believed they would succeed in muddling through.

"Be nice to play diplomat for a change, eh, Spock?"

Dead silence.

"Look, Spock," he continued, turning in the chair, "I know you find the hypocritical methodology of interstellar diplomacy somewhat obscene, but that shouldn't prevent you from enjoying the fringe bene—"

Without a word, without a sound, without a shift in

expression or pose, Spock abruptly toppled over and crashed to the floor.

Kirk was quite capable of reacting quickly and efficiently to anything from the sudden appearance of half a dozen belligerent warships on the fore screen to impending dissolution of the *Enterprise*, from the sight of a being a hundred times larger than the ship to an entire metropolis no bigger than the bridge. But Spock's collapse was so totally unexpected, so deathly quiet and matter-of-fact, that for one of the few times during his tenure as commanding officer of the *Enterprise* he found himself momentarily paralyzed.

Even so, he recovered before any of the other equally stunned crew. A hand slammed down on the intercom switch.

"Kirk to Sick Bay—Bones, we've got an emergency."

While seemingly hours passed without aid appearing, they fought to control their feelings and do what they could. There wasn't much they *could* do, beyond untangling the first officer's crumpled limbs and laying him flat on the deck—and wondering what the heck had happened. Kirk had put an ear to Spock's chest and found temporary relief in the steady beat of a Vulcan heart. But no amount of exterior stimulation—or pleading—could return Spock to consciousness.

McCoy finally appeared, a mobile surgical bed and two medical techs in tow. Kneeling over the still form, he made a quick pass over head and torso with a portable medical transceiver, then directed the pair of assistants as they laid the motionless Spock on the bed.

Kirk followed them out, knowing better than to trouble McCoy with dozens of as yet unanswerable questions. As soon as answers were available, the good doctor would supply them without having to be asked.

On reaching Sick Bay, McCoy had Spock transferred from the mobile pallet to one of the much better equipped diagnostic beds. While the doctor smoothly adjusted the requisite instrumentation for Vulcan physiology, Kirk hovered nearby, watching, waiting for a determination of some sort. Kirk knew something about every instrument and machine on board the *Enterprise*, but many of the figures which blossomed on the glowing panel above the bed head meant little to him. Those whose meaning he could vaguely identify seemed to indicate the presence of an uncommon abnormality within the science officer's system.

McCoy prepared and administered a hastily concocted injection. Only when the applied serum took did he appear to relax slightly.

"I brought him out of shock, Jim," he finally said. "He's sleeping normally now. Choriocytosis is a strange disease. It's relatively simple to handle in races with iron-based blood, but in others . . ."

A warning tingle started in Kirk's mind.

"Get to the point, Bones."

McCoy appeared to consider something else for a moment, shook it off and eyed Kirk steadily. "Spock has contracted the disease. It's a nuisance to humans. To Vulcans it's fatal. Ninety-three percent probability, as—" his words slowed and finished almost imperceptibly "—Spock would say."

Kirk cleared his throat. "You're sure it's choriocytosis?"

"I've triple-checked, Jim, given the instrumentation every opportunity to prove me wrong." He shrugged helplessly. "I wish to God I was wrong, but you can see it eating at him. Look . . ."

He urged Kirk to activate a nearby view screen. While the captain did so, McCoy went to a cabinet. Selecting a tiny cassette, he slid it into a slot beneath the glowing screen, punched out commands on the operating panel.

A few seconds of blurred images raced across the screen as the cassette ran up to the place McCoy had requested. It slowed and commenced normal playback. You didn't need a medical degree to understand what was happening. One sequence stayed with Kirk long after he had left Sick Bay.

It showed a collage of healthy, green-tinted Vulcan cells. From screen right, a flowing yellowish substance slid like sapient gelatin into view. It divided, subdivided, to surround each individual cell. On being engulfed, the afflicted cells started to jerk unnaturally, their steady movements interrupted. Healthy green deepened to light blue, then azure, almost to purple before all internal motion ceased and cellular disruption took place.

On that threatening note, the tape ran out.

McCoy slid the casette free, juggled it idly in one hand, flipping it over and over as he spoke.

"The sequences you say, Jim, were highly speeded up. Simply, the infection enters the blood and affects the cells so that they can't carry oxygen. For some reason, iron-based hemoglobin fights off the encirclement much better than copper-based. I wish I knew why. The result is obvious."

"Eventual collapse," Kirk supplied softly.

McCoy quit flipping the casette, put it back in its place in the cabinet then closed the sliding door with more force than was necessary.

"That's it, Jim."

"You said ninety-three percent probability of death, Bones. What about that other seven percent? Does that mean there's a cure?"

"Not always. But there's a drug that would certainly improve the odds in Spock's favor astronomically—if we could get it."

"We'll get it," Kirk told him. His reply would have been the same if McCoy had requested the heart of a dead sun.

"It's a naturally occurring drug called strobolin. Sixty years in the lab and nobody's been able to synthesize it. It's a rare drug, Jim, but choriocytosis is a rare disease."

Kirk nodded, moved for the switch that would open the wall intercom and connect him to the bridge. Then something that had been scratching at the back of his mind finally broke through.

"Bones, if you knew we were experiencing an outbreak of choriocytosis on board and that it could be fatal to Spock if he contracted it—why didn't you order him into isolation until the disease burned itself out?"

McCoy looked away. "I didn't want to have to tell you, Jim."

"Didn't want to have to tell me what, Bones?" Kirk shot back, a little angry. "What could anything have to do with not telling me?"

"I said choriocytosis was a rare disease. My guess is your system was laid open to it—" he looked back, "—by the multiple alterations your circulatory system was subjected to while on Argo. In which case—"

"You didn't want to tell me that Spock and I had infected the whole ship." McCoy nodded, watched the captain anxiously. But Kirk appeared to bear up well under a revelation that might have affected a lesser man dangerously.

"Then, why did I and plenty of others get sick, go through the disease and get cured, and then all of a sudden Spock collapses?"

McCoy looked tired. "Incubation period, Jim. It's a lot longer for Vulcans than for humans. There was no point in telling Spock, nothing to be gained. If he had it, there wasn't a thing I could do about it."

"Why is the incubation period so much?" Kirk began, but McCoy cut him off angrily, his voice rising.

"Why, why, why, why! If I knew the answers to all the whys, choriocytosis wouldn't *be* such a putrid, disgusting—"

"Sorry, Bones," Kirk interrupted softly. There wasn't much else he could say. McCoy'd only been expressing the same frustration he felt.

Instead he activated the nearby computer annex. "Library!"

"Awaiting input," came the instant, mechanical reply.

"What is the nearest strobolin supply world to our present position?"

"Canopus Two," the library responded promptly. "Four days distant at maximum warp."

Kirk flipped off the annex and headed for the door, then stopped in mid-stride and returned, to stare down at the corpselike—no, not corpselike, he hurriedly corrected himself—the sleeping form of Spock.

"How long can he last without the drug?"

McCoy considered carefully, his momentary outburst already forgotten by both men. "I said strobolin couldn't be duplicated in the lab. That's so—but there is an artificially produced related serum I ought to be able to make up.

"All it can do is slow the disease, not stop it. The destructive agent rapidly builds an immunity to the serum. Despite all forestalling efforts, at the rate his blood is losing the ability to carry oxygen, I give him three days at best, Jim. Four days to reach the drug—and Spock will die in three in spite of everything I can do. That's," an odd expression came over him, "logical. Unless—"

"Unless what, Bones?"

McCoy looked guarded. "What about a rendezvous?"

"Of course! If we can't reach the drug in time, there's a chance that another Federation ship might be close to Canopus Two right now. There's *got* to be!" He was back at the intercom in seconds.

"Kirk to Bridge—get me Starfleet operations control for this sector, Lieutenant."

"Transmitting, Captain."

The logistics seemed beyond immediate solution. However, it was startling how much bureaucracy and red tape one could cut through by bringing the proper amount of priority demands, prime requests and insinuations to bear—all seasoned with a touch of judicious threats.

It was eventually decided that the starship *Potemkin*, presently on patrol in the region of Canopus, would pick up the requisite amount of strobolin. This would then be transferred to the interstellar freighter *Huron* for delivery to the *Enterprise*.

Kirk would have preferred meeting the *Potemkin* himself and avoiding any intermediaries. But there were certain requests even he couldn't have filled—tying up two starships for speedy delivery of a drug was one of them.

Spock was a valued officer—but he was only one. Starfleet had a plethora of personnel and a distinct shortage of starships. Vessels the class of the *Enterprise* and *Potemkin* were too few and far between for their missions to be casually aborted—or so said the reply to his request.

Kirk didn't argue with the logic of the missive, but the word "casual" in reference to Spock filled him with a quiet hatred for some unknown officer whose career had been spent behind a desk pushing paper.

On the other hand, if all went well they would still receive the drug in plenty of time. And McCoy had assured him that strobolin's effectiveness matched its rarity.

McCoy leaned against the wall in Kirk's cabin and watched his superior officer and good friend going through mental nip-ups. With the exception of Spock, he was probably the only one on board who knew that this was the first time Kirk had ever traded on his reputation to produce desired results.

Kirk hated officers who used "pull" to get what they wanted. So his embarrassment at doing so himself was understandable. McCoy repressed a smile. If the captain only knew the awe the rest of the crew held him in for being able to generate such action on the part of a notoriously somnolent bureaucracy.

Naturally no one showed the admiration they felt—everyone knew it would only embarrass him more.

As for himself, he mused exhaustedly, he had done everything it was humanly—or for that matter, Vulcanly—possible to do for the mortally ill first officer. Now he must devote his energies to ensuring that Kirk wouldn't fold up as the critical rendezvous approached. The last thing he wanted was *two* important patients.

"What are the symptoms like, Bones?" Kirk finally muttered idly, staring at the ceiling. The three-dimensional desert diorama projected above his bed offered little comfort.

McCoy shrugged, tried to make the terrifying sound casual. "Increasing difficulty in breathing, coupled with a corresponding drop in efficiency. All the signs of someone working under extreme altitude conditions. Kind of like the standard Academy mountain survival test. Remember that one?"

That memory produced a small grin ... very small. It vanished when the door buzzer sounded politely.

"Come."

The panel slid aside, and the subject of all the recent activity walked in. Spock showed no sign of the concern or trouble centering on him. His uniform and posture were immaculate, as usual. His expression was bland as vanilla, as usual. Only in his movements could one who knew him well detect something amiss. Lift of hand, drive of leg, all were just a hair slow, the movements of a man recently arisen from a deep sleep.

Or slipping into one, Kirk thought morosely.

"You wish to see me, Captain?"

"Yes, Spock. Sit down."

With a quick glance at McCoy, who in trying to avoid it only made his concern more obvious, Spock took up a seat facing Kirk. The captain swung his legs off the bed, sat up.

"We've arranged a rendezvous to pick up the drug you need."

"I trust it will not affect our scheduled arrival at Deneb Five, nor our duties there?"

"No, it won't," Kirk said gently.

"What's the matter, Spock?" put in McCoy in a forced attempt at levity, "afraid you'll miss the first dance at the Federation Academy ball?"

"I'm afraid I do not dance, Doctor."

"You can say that again," McCoy countered, but he did it without a smile and the attempted joke fell flat.

An awkward pause ensued while Kirk considered how to proceed. With any other member of the crew he wouldn't have had to. But could he simply say what had to be said to Spock? The first officer perceived certain things differently than others. Would he be offended? Angry? More than anything else, Kirk wished now he knew more about Vulcan customs—and etiquette, in particular.

"Will that be all, Captain?" Spock asked, giving Kirk no more time to hope for divine intervention.

"One more thing, Spock," he began, without meeting his first officer's gaze. "I've considered very carefully. Based on Dr. McCoy's recommendations—(*that's it, make Bones the heavy, James T. Chicken*)—*I've* decided to cut your duty time in half."

A faint glimmer of something close to emotion seemed to shine behind dark pupils. "Captain, that won't be necessary. I am perfectly capable of . . ."

A hand came down on his shoulder and he glanced around and up. McCoy, firm, not joking now.

"No argument, Spock. Doctor's orders."

Kirk watched his first officer carefully. No reaction. Of course not—a sign of health in itself.

"That's all, Spock," he said curtly, before his friend could offer additional rejoinders. "Dismissed."

Spock nodded once, rose and walked slowly to the door. McCoy relaxed perceptibly as soon as the portal closed behind him.

"Whew. He took that better than I expected."

"He took it like Spock—no, that's not fair of me, Bones."

"Forget it, Jim. I know how you feel—it's hard, watching him like that and waiting for the collapse you know is coming. I just wish there was something more I could do for him."

"It'll hurt seeing him go steadily downhill."

McCoy looked philosophical. "The only other alternative is to confine him to quarters, or to Sick Bay. I don't see any point in that. It won't do anything for him from a physical standpoint and it could only hurt him mentally. So I see no harm in letting him—"

"Feel useful in his last hours?"

Both men stared quietly at each other, each lost in his own thoughts—the strongest presence in the room that of one who was no longer there.

Streamlining had given way to functionality in the latter part of the Twenty-First Century. So the ships which carried freight between the stars were equal parts ugly and efficient, ungainly and profitable.

The S. S. Huron was typical if this class and its crew typical of crews on such ships. There were some who insisted that the small living quarters on board such craft made for small men. In reality, the reverse was usually true. They were no less daring, no less brave than starship personnel—only sloppier and more independent.

Captain O'Shea of the Huron probably fell about midway between fiction and reality. Outwardly there was little to distinguish him. He was of average build

and temperament, excepting the special sole of his left
shoe, constructed to accommodate the fact that the one
leg was a number of centimeters shorter than the other
one. On such minutiae do careers in Starfleet hang.

Naturally, that detail made him stronger than those
he was passed over in favor of. O'Shea needed that
strength. The duller the task, the more inner strength a
man needed to survive.

His face, at least, was noble, adequately laden with
planes and angles inscribed by years of service. It
might have been taken from the bust of a Roman patri-
cian, despite the incongruity of the five-o'clock shadow.

At the moment he stood in the small, curved chamber which served as the bridge for the *Huron*. His two
assistants were seated before him at the compact control console, staring at the fore viewscreen.

Quarters were snug. On board a freighter everything
was sacrificed for the comfort of the cargo. O'Shea and
his crew were classed with the other incidental equipment.

"Time to rendezvous . . . ," Elijah paused briefly to
check a readout, ". . . two hours seven minutes, Captain."

O'Shea grunted in acknowledgment. It was his favor-
ite mode of expression, being at once eloquent and
economical. He also had an excellent negative grunt.
O'Shea could produce a veritable spectrum, an *olla po-
drida* of grunts, constituting a language in themselves.

But the unusual importance of this run compared to
their usual assignments compelled him to greater loqua-
ciousness, his ambivalent feelings about the job not-
withstanding.

"Must be a pretty important drug we're carrying for
the *Enterprise*. I'd just as soon get rid of it and get back
to shipping plain dilithium."

The *Huron*'s first officer, John Elijah, smiled to himself. Despite his constant complaining, he knew O'Shea
was reveling in the attention they had received. The
captain had been hard-pressed to keep the seams of his
jacket intact when the priority call had come through
from Starfleet, with its companion orders.

O'Shea already had had a chance to do a little strutting before the crew of the *Potemkin*. Now he was looking forward to playing hero before the officers of one of the most famous ships in the Federation, the *Enterprise*.

No wonder he was feeling talkative!

He felt a tap on his arm and looked across at his partner. Lieutenant Fushi eyed him questioningly, directed his attention to a certain readout on the other side of the console. Like nearly everything else, the by-play caught O'Shea's attention.

"What are you two on about?"

"Sir," Fushi confessed, openly puzzled, "our sensors are registering the presence of a ship ahead." Several intriguing new crevices appeared in the captain's mobile face.

"Odd. Could the *Enterprise* be this early? Sure, and this is listed as a priority meeting, but . . ."

"Still too far away to tell what it is, sir," Fushi replied.

"What's its approximate course?"

"Toward us, sir."

O'Shea grunted. Elijah and Fushi had no trouble translating it to, "Well, that's all very interesting information Lieutenant, and I certainly hope it is the *Enterprise*; but since we're not sure yet perhaps you'd best keep an eye on it."

In the hands of a master like the captain the content of a barely verbalized monosyllable could be truly startling.

Kirk halted dictation into his private log and looked to the helm. "Time to rendezvous, Mr. Arex?"

The Edoan checked the chronometer readout, compared it with the declaration of another gauge. "One hour forty-three minutes, Captain."

Kirk considered this briefly before turning his attention to the Bridge engineering station, where Scott was keeping a close watch on numerous gauges.

"Scotty, I hate to ask this, but . . ."

Scott simply looked back and nodded. "Aye, Captain, we'll squeeze a bit more speed out of her somehow."

"If it'll help, Scotty, I'll get out and push."

"Any of us would, Captain. Let me see what I can do."

An insistent buzz pulled Kirk's attention back to the chair intercom.

"McCoy to bridge."

Kirk opened the channel. "What is it, Bones?"

"Tell Spock it's time for another shot."

Kirk lowered his voice as he looked over toward the science station. "Again, Bones?"

"Again, Jim."

Kirk sighed. "All right, I'll send him down." He raised his voice. "Mr. Spock." There was no response. "Mr. Spock!" Now Sulu had turned to stare, and Uhura had swiveled 'round at her station.

"He looks tired, Bones," Kirk said into the pickup. "Just a minute." He got out of the chair and walked toward his first officer. "Spock? Spock!"

The first officer's eyes, which had been closed as Kirk approached, opened slowly. He gazed blankly up at Kirk for a moment. Then both eyes and mind seemed to clear simultaneously.

"I was conserving energy, Captain."

Kirk nodded matter-of-factly, trying not to let his relief show. "McCoy wants you in Sick Bay. Time for another injection."

Spock rose from his seat—slowly, carefully, but without aid—and walked toward the elevator with the same measured movements.

The silence on the bridge was deafening.

O'Shea leaned between his two juniors and studied the abstract overlay on the viewscreen. So far it could show no more than a moving blip—enigmatic and uniformly uninformative.

Fushi had been staring into a gooseneck viewer for long moments. Now he sat back, flipped a single switch and rubbed his eyes. He had collated the mass approximations, extreme-range silhouette configuration estimates, energy registration and a dozen others. These enabled him to make a single terse announcement.

"It's not the *Enterprise* closing on us, sir."

"Another Federation vessel?" There was more hope than confidence in O'Shea's voice now.

"No, sir. It's an outsider for sure. A design I don't recognize. That's not to say half the helmsmen in the Federation wouldn't recognize it, but *I* don't."

"That's good enough for me," O'Shea acknowledged grimly. "Are we close enough yet for visual pickup?"

"Three minutes on our current course should bring it within range of our fore telescanners, sir."

O'Shea considered. From the beginning he'd enjoyed this mission. It had provided a chance for some infrequent recognition as well as an opportunity to present himself as a person of importance. Everything had run smoothly.

Now there was a loose neutron in the reaction chamber, and he found he didn't like it one bit.

Fushi was doing his best with the *Huron*'s telescopic pickups. The abstract overlay vanished from the main screen, to be replaced by a wavering, fuzzy starfield. In its center was what appeared at first glance to be a red star.

Fushi made adjustments, and the star became a ship. O'Shea studied the unknown visitor intently. Its design was different, but not extreme—alien without being radical. It was colored blood red, a choice which might be coincidental, theatrical, or intentional.

One out o' three, he mused, ain't good.

"You sure it's coming toward us?" he asked again.

Eiljah was busy checking gauges. "Definitely on an intercept course, Captain. Estimates of speed . . . it'll reach us before we make contact with the *Enterprise*."

"Maybe," said Fushi quietly, "they just want to chat."

"Maybe," agreed O'Shea, staring at the alien image as it grew nearer and nearer. "Maybe . . ."

"Maybe we can dispense with these injections soon, Spock," McCoy told him.

Spock was lying down on one of the diagnostic beds. Nurse Chapel stood nearby. McCoy wielded the air hypo like an artist with a brush, placed it against the first officer's shoulder.

"This won't hurt a bit now, Spock."

"An unnecessary reassurance, Doctor," his patient replied, "in addition to being untrue."

McCoy grimaced as he administered the serum. "That's the last time I waste my best bedside manner on a Vulcan."

Spock, rolling down the sleeve of his tunic, started to sit up. "Such restraint would be welcome, Doctor."

McCoy put a hand on the first officer's untreated shoulder and gently pressed him back. "Agreed, provided you show some of the same, Spock. Lie there quietly."

Nodding to Chapel, he directed his full attention to the screen over the head of the bed. Chapel adjusted the complex diagnostic mechanism. The result was a series of brightly lit printouts on the screen which the patient, in his reclining position, couldn't see.

Respiration, circulation—McCoy went through the succession of figures, compared them with those taken four hours earlier. There was nothing there he hadn't expected to see. That made them no less depressing.

Considering the massive doses Spock had been receiving, one would think those strobolin analogs would be more effective. To an observer basing his opinion on the present readings, all those injections would seem to have been worse than useless.

But McCoy knew that without those injections he would not be reading any results on Spock now. Corpses generate singularly uniform figures. He looked down at the subject of all this analysis, who waited patiently for permission to get back to his assigned tasks, and smiled in manner belying his true feelings.

"Well, that's not too bad . . . not too bad at all. I'm afraid it's back to the salt mines for you, Spock."

Spock started to get up, nearly fell. McCoy managed to restrain himself to the barest twitch and kept himself from extending a supportive arm.

"Thank you, Doctor," Spock said evenly, getting to his feet slowly but steadily now. Like a man in a dream, he left the room.

Chapel's professional smile didn't fade until he was gone. "The drug isn't working any more, Doctor. If it was, he wouldn't have lost that much ground in four hours." McCoy turned from her, troubled.

"I know, Christine, I know. The additional injections can't hurt his system and psychologically they may help. Don't worry . . . we'll have the strobolin soon."

That was what McCoy said. But a person did not have to be as familiar with him as Chapel was to read what he meant.

They'd *better* have the strobolin soon . . .

"They've increased speed, sir," Fushi reported tightly. "Closing fast on us now."

"Why do I have this nagging impression they want more from us than just talk?" O'Shea muttered. "Open hailing frequencies, Mr. Elijah. Standard intership call."

The first officer of the *Huron* reached for the required instruments, manipulated several. "Open, sir. They're plenty close enough; should pick us up easy."

O'Shea moved forward, spoke toward the directional mike.

"To unidentified alien vessel. This is Captain Svenquist O'Shea of the Federation freighter *S.S. Huron*—on whose course you are currently closing. Please state your registry and intentions." He paused, repeated, "Please identify yourself."

"No use, sir," a vexed Elijah reported. "They've got to be receiving . . . but they're not answering."

Well, that left two possibilities. The first was that the stranger was in sufficient difficulties to render his broadcast instrumentation inoperative.

The second was that O'Shea was in a lot of trouble and needed help, but fast.

"We've got a hold full of dilithium to protect, not to mention that drug," he ventured. "I don't like people who come at me fast and silent. Evasive maneuvers."

Fushi and Elijah were good. They tried right-left angle shifts. They put the *Huron* through turns warp-drive craft weren't designed for. They sent her galloping off course in a random-number spiral.

None of it fazed their silent pursuer. Whatever sought close contact with them was simply too fast to be denied. Time and again it would slip off the *Huron*'s screens, only to reappear moments later. And with each new maneuver tried, each option exhausted, the alien grew harder and harder to shake. Their pilots might not have been any better—but their navigational computer and engines were clearly designed for more intricate work than traveling from point *A* to point *B*.

"It's no good, sir," a tired Fushi confessed. "Not only can't we lose them, they're still closing on us."

"All right." O'Shea was running down a list of responses to possible challenges. "Resume course, and send out an emergency signal to the *Enterprise*. By drone. Subtly."

"Yes, sir." He programed the drone properly, sent it on its robotic way. "Might be a good idea to ready a backup, in case." His hands moved to make the necessary demands on the *Huron*'s equipment—and hesitated as a certain telltale commenced a steady winking.

"Message coming in, sir."

"I can see that, man. Let's hear it."

Elijah acknowledged the call, put it on the speaker. They had cut in mid-broadcast.

It didn't matter. The message directed at them was as understandable as it was incomplete.

". . . or prepare to be destroyed. Stand by to surrender your cargo or prepare . . ."

VII

"Captain, I'm getting a signal from the *Huron*—by automatic emergency beacon."

Kirk stiffened in his seat. "Are we close enough for direct ship-to-ship contact yet?"

Uhura checked a readout. "Possible, sir—fringe tangency."

"Try it."

"Yes, sir." There was a pause, then, "Nothing, sir. Either we're still too far off or—it's definitely an emergency beacon doing the broadcasting." She didn't have to elaborate.

"Sensor report, Mr. Spock. Have they reached the designated coordinates?" It took Spock several seconds longer than usual to make the check and reply.

"No, sir. Long-range scanners also indicate a course change. They are veering off—and have reduced speed considerably."

"Compute new course to intercept, Mr. Arex. Lieutenant Uhura, keep trying to make contact. Let's find out what's going on—"

It took longer than Kirk expected to make the rendezvous, not because of the course change but because the *Huron* had not merely cut speed—she had practically stopped.

Visual contact soon revealed the reasons why. The freighter sat there on the main viewscreen, drifting aimlessly in space. All entreaties for acknowledgment were ignored with frightening uniformity.

Spock's attention was on his hooded viewer. "The *Huron*'s power levels are functioning at the bare minimum required to maintain life-support systems, Captain. And sensors are picking up considerable metallic and other inorganic debris."

"Natural cause?"

Spock looked up from the viewer. "No, Captain. Extrapolating from preliminary data I would say without qualification that she was attacked. Indications are ... indications are ..." He swayed in his chair, eyelids fluttering.

"Spock!"

For a moment the first officer's eyes opened wide and clear. Then a faint suggestion of uncertainty crossed that stolid visage. "Captain, I ..."

Kirk started forward—caught the limp form before it struck the floor. Uhura was already on the intercom.

"Bridge to Sick Bay—*Emergency!*"

Kirk felt no need to ask McCoy for a detailed interpretation of the readings that winked on and off on the screen above Spock's head. Anyone with a minimal knowledge of Vulcan physiology could see that they were appallingly low.

McCoy studied he unconscious Vulcan. "We've got to have that strobolin, Jim. The synthetic is useless now—hell, it's been useless for half a day! He has lapsed into coma." He looked unwaveringly at Kirk.

"If we don't get that drug soon, very soon, he'll never come out of it."

"Do what you can, Bones." It sounded pitifully inadequate. "And I'll—I'll do what *I* can."

Now they had another problem to cope with. What had happened to the *Huron*? He gave McCoy a hesitant, encouraging pat on the back and left Sick Bay.

McCoy watched him go, his one note of satisfaction in this being Kirk's continued steadiness; then he turned his attention back to his patient. He examined the readouts again. For the moment they were unchanged. Temporary, false pleasure—they could only change for the worse.

"Blasted Vulcan!" he yelled at the motionless form, "Why couldn't you have red blood like any normal man?"

He prayed for a comforting insult.

He got only sibilant breathing—and silence.

Arex was manning Spock's station as Sulu positioned the *Enterprise* close to the unresponsive *Huron*.

"Status?" Kirk queried sharply, striding out of the elevator.

"Her engines are dead," Arex reported, studying the telltale sensor screen. "Backup battery power is operating life-support systems at a low but acceptable level."

"Anyone left alive?"

"There appears to be, sir. Several weak readings. I can't tell how many for certain."

"We'll find out soon enough. Mr. Scott, Lieutenant Uhura, come with me. Mr. Sulu, you have the con. We're beaming over to the *Huron*."

Dissolution ... nausea ... teasing oblivion ... reassembly.

Kirk looked around and saw that Kyle had put them exactly where he had specified. They were standing on the *Huron*'s bridge. Or rather, on what was left of it.

It looked as if something had taken the *Huron* by its stern and slammed the upper end against a nickel-iron asteroid. Signs of severe concussion were everywhere—in the shattered gauge covers, the slight ooze of liquid around loosened paneling from cracked fluid-state switches, in the decided chill in the air from the release of super-cooled gases.

Further evidence was to be found in the condition of two of the three skulls belonging to the crew.

Chapel made a quick examination of the physical damage and tended to Fushi, the most severely injured of the three, first. Whatever had battered the *Huron* had made no distinction between accouterments living and dead. Her three officers were scattered about the bridge with the same disregard and in the same condition as the furnishings.

Kirk waited with agonized impatience as Chapel moved quickly from Fushi to O'Shea to Elijah.

"They'll all live," she said finally. Kirk turned.

"Scotty, check the cargo hold for the strobolin. Every freighter has a double-walled refrigerated chamber for storing extremely valuable cargo. It should be located close by the central accessway. The drug will be in it."

"Aye, sir." Scott turned, started back into the bowels of the ship.

"Uhura, see if you can get a playback off their log. I want to know what happened here."

Uhura nodded, moved to the chaos of the fore control console and commenced trying to make sense out of the tangle of wiring, torn metal and shredded plastics.

Kirk examined what was left of the small engineering station, wished Scotty were around to explain the destruction. Whatever had ruined the freighter had been guided by an intelligence with a definite purpose in mind. The damage here was severe—but still controlled. Something had disabled the freighter without destroying it.

It was difficult to fault their thoroughness. True, they had left O'Shea and his crew alive—barely. But there was no reason to expect three severely wounded men drifting powerless in a little-frequented section of space and existing on stored energy to ever be rescued and bear witness against their attacker.

No, the *Huron* might very well have gone down on shipping schedules as just one of those infrequent vessels marked "never arrived—cause unknown," if it weren't for the fact that the ship was to meet the oncoming *Enterprise* in free space. Something Kirk doubted her attackers had known, or they would have taken care to leave no one alive. They had made a mistake.

Possibly a fatal one.

There was a buzz close by, and Kirk flipped on his communicator.

"Scott to Captain Kirk," the familiar voice of the chief engineer came. Kirk glanced around the shattered bridge. Chapel had turned her ministrations to O'Shea. Uhura deftly avoided a sudden shower of sparks, then bent with renewed vigor to the task of extricating the remnants of the *Huron's* log.

"Kirk here . . . all steady forward, Scotty. Report."

"I'm in the main bay, Captain. The *Huron's* equipped with a security bin, all right—only it's been forced.

It's as empty as the rest of the cargo hold. There's nothin' down here, Captain."

"No sign of the strobolin?"

"Not a single ampoule, Captain. The *Huron's* listed cargo for this trip was dilithium. Not a crystal in sight, either. The hold's been stripped clean."

"Life-support systems?"

"Stable here. No, if this was caused by a natural disaster it's been repaired with the slickest patch job I've ever seen. Also, it must have been a mighty selective disaster. The only major damage is to the security chamber and the cargo locks. I kinna tell for sure from this distance, but I think they were blown open and then resealed."

"All right, Mr. Scott. Report back up here."

"Aye, Sir. Sorry I am . . ."

No drug, a voice howled in Kirk's mind. No drug, no drug! He flipped off the communicator and walked over next to the busy Uhura. She looked up at him and wiped a forearm across her brow. The humidity was bad in here and getting worse, despite the valiant efforts of the damaged life-support system.

"All recorders are gone, sir—but indications are that the log tapes are intact. I think I can extricate them without damage. We'll have to play them back on board ship, though."

"Good enough, Lieutenant." He left her to her work and turned his attention back to Chapel. She continued to labor on O'Shea.

"How is he, Nurse?"

"Scrambled inside, concussion upstairs—he needs surgery but," she smiled slightly, "he'll live, Captain. Nothing we can't fix. Another couple of days, though, and all three of them would have been gone."

Kirk moved away, thinking hard. He flipped the communicator open again just as Scott re-entered the bridge.

"Kirk to *Enterprise*. We're ready to beam over, Arex. Have a full medical team standing by. We need—" he glanced at Chapel, who nodded approval as he spoke, "—three pallets with tech-teams. Tell Dr. McCoy he's got a triple surgery on his hands."

"Very good, sir," the thin voice piped back.

They left the *Huron* where and as it was, it's automatic beacon still calling plaintively to an indifferent universe. Scott had installed a fully charged power pack to run the beacon when the freighter's emergency batteries finally gave out.

The shattered transport could be recovered later, by someone else. Right now something other than salvage dominated Kirk's thoughts. And Scott's, and McCoy's, and Sulu's—and those of every other member of the *Enterprise*'s crew—though they might not have admitted it.

Such thoughts were doubtlessly the cause of the pounding headache Kirk suffered from as he paced the outer room of the Sick Bay. His attention was gratefully drawn from the miners excavating his skull when McCoy entered from a side doorway. The reflective figure, clad in transparent surgical garb, beckoned Kirk to a familiar chamber.

Kirk walked past the base of the bed where Spock lay immobile. He glanced once at the diagnostic readouts on the screen above, looked hurriedly away. By now even the figures were painful to see.

He turned in time to see O'Shea wheeled in from surgery. Two medical techs transferred the *Huron*'s captain gently from the mobile pallet to a duplicate of the bed Spock lay in.

Both officers walked over, McCoy peeling the protective sealer from his face. "How's this one, Bones?"

"Oh, he'll pull through all right, Jim. Just a little rearrangement of his plumbing . . . no permanent damage." He paused. "Jim, what the hell are we going to do about Spock?"

"The best we can, Bones."

"I'm not sure that's going to be good enough, Jim."

Kirk could see that McCoy was sorry for the words as soon as he had said them. He was under more pressure than anyone else on board just now, and it manifested itself as frustration.

Probably there was nothing as agonizing to a doctor of Bones' ability as knowing exactly what to do to cure

a patient and simply not having the material to do it
with.

"If we don't have that strobolin in twenty hours,
he'll die," McCoy continued flatly. "That's a minimal
figure, but it's pretty accurate. I wouldn't like to have
to stretch it even five minutes."

There was nothing he could say . . . just as there was
nothing he could do.

No, no—that wasn't entirely true. There was still a
chance, still some hope. The dimness of the readings on
the diagnostic indicators over Spock's head were
matched by the snail's pace of his thoughts.

"We still might—"

"Might what, Jim?"

"Wait till I see the log tapes we took off the *Huron*.
If they're wiped, or if the recorder was destroyed too
soon—" He stopped abruptly. "See you later, Bones.
Do what you can for Spock, and let me know the minute any of those three," he nodded to where Elijah was
being brought in to join O'Shea, "recover sufficiently to
talk."

Never enough time, he thought, never enough . . .

As Arex ran the *Huron* tapes through the library
computer, Kirk stood nearby and urged the dawdling
computer to faster action.

Eventually, the Edoan made his equivalent of a satisfied sigh. "Some of the last tape was burned, Captain.
I've been able to reconstruct the damaged sections,
however. The *Huron* was definitely, as we suspected,
attacked by another vessel. It is interesting to observe
that the belligerent ship is a new design, one apparently
never before encountered by a Federation ship. There
is also evidence to suggest that it possesses an older
form of propulsion than modern warp drive."

"I don't care if it came from the far side of M one
one three eight and is powered by ten million invisible
gerbils—all I want to know is, can we track it?"

"That's the significance of its out-of-date drive, sir.
If you'll look here . . ."

He hit a switch. Immediately a blank grid appeared
on the small screen above the science console. Another

control produced a star-chart nearby. Arex made a last adjustment and the two blended together.

Kirk squinted. There were glowing dots on the composite screen which were not stars.

"The *Huron*'s attacker may be sophisticated in many ways," Arex explained, "but its propulsive units are possessed of a few archaic features. One of these is that they generate a faint residue of radioactive particulate matter. Unless they are aware of us and have carefully laid a false trail for us to follow—which I strongly doubt—we should be able to find them.

"The most recent deposits give a bearing of two hundred twelve plus, one hundred seventy-five minus to the Galactic ecliptic. The half-life of the ejected material is quite short. If we had arrived on the scene as much as three days late, our sensors would have found nothing."

"Lay in that course!" Kirk shouted back to the helm. "Ahead warp seven, Mr. Sulu." He turned back to Arex. "Run through those tapes again—slowly, Lieutenant—and let me know if you find anything else you think significant. I'll be down in Sick Bay."

Kirk found McCoy seated at his desk, his head resting in his hands. "How is he, Bones."

"Worse than he was when you left, Jim," McCoy replied, looking up. "And he'll be worse the next time, and worse after that . . . until we get that drug.

"It's his breathing that worries me most. Pretty soon I'm going to have to put him on forced respiration. That'll draw reserves from other parts of his body already hard-pressed by the disease."

"Well, we're following the attacking ship's trail." Teeth gleamed. "We're going to crawl right up—"

"Ship?" McCoy interrupted. "How do we know there's only one ship involved in this?"

"Lieutenant Arex is certain the radioactive residue comes from a single vessel."

"Sure, only one ship *attacked* the *Huron*. What happens if they rendezvous with another and transfer cargo? Or with two others, or make multiple transfers?"

"Dammit, Bones," Kirk half shouted, "this one's got

to be the *only* one. It's *got* to be." McCoy looked apologetic, but Kirk waved off the incipient sorrys.

"Don't complicate things with factual possibilities, okay? If there's more than one ship, well ... that's probably it, then. We haven't enough time to go chasing all over the cosmos after several ships, even if their trails would last that long."

"A transfer," McCoy finished relentlessly, "would seem the logical thing to do." His voice cracked on the word "logical."

"Sure, *if* you anticipate immediate pursuit. But every sign points to these beings—whoever they are—not expecting another vessel in this region. Certainly not one capable of overtaking them.

"The tapes indicate they weren't much on conversation. Chances are that if O'Shea had been given the opportunity to explain he was about to rendezvous with a heavy cruiser, they might have called off the whole thing."

"I'm sure that'll be a great consolation to O'Shea when he comes around," snorted McCoy. He walked slowly back to stare down at Spock.

"What's the good of being a physician, anyway?" Kirk heard him mutter angrily. "We're only as good as current drugs and technology make us. We've got a few more books, a little more knowledge. Eliminate all the mechanical conveniences, and I might as well be practicing in the middle ages. There's nothing *I* can do for him." He walked a few steps away, slammed a hand against the door sill.

"Me—me, I'm helpless. Totally dependent on instrumentation and pre-programed chemicals. There isn't a thing *I* personally can do. So what's the point of it—what's the point?" He stared down at the floor.

"Better to be an engineer like Scotty. If one of his patients burns out, there's always a replacement in the catalog." A hollow laugh forced itself out.

Silence.

Then, "If you really believed that, Bones," Kirk told him softly, "you wouldn't still be a doctor after twenty-five years. *Especially* a ship's doctor.

"And that's something else I've always wondered

about, Bones. Why did you bother entering the service? With your skill you could have made a fortune in government or private practice."

McCoy glanced back sharply, an unfathomable expression on his face. "You're going to find this funny, Jim, but . . . I entered the service instead of striking out on my own because I'm greedy."

"Greedy?" As Spock would say, that sounds like an irrefutable contradiction in terms."

McCoy shook his head. "It's no different for me than for you, Jim. I'm here because challenge means more to me than money. And because money can't buy a sense of accomplishment.

"Besides, could you see me sitting in a private clinic on Demolos or on Earth, pandering to the private phobias of overweight matrons and spoiled kids?"

"I admit it's a tough scene to picture," Kirk agreed, amused. "I'm glad your avarice drove you to become doctor on this ship."

"Listen," McCoy began, "if Spock pulls through—"

"You mean *when* Spock pulls through," Kirk countered forcefully. "When Spock pulls through I'll see what can be done about rounding up some more interesting illnesses for you to play with. I don't want you feeling unchallenged."

"Thanks awfully, Jim," McCoy responded, a touch of his normal sarcasm coming back. "I'd appreciate some really different germs for a change. Trouble is, the people on this ship refuse to cooperate. You're all too damned healthy."

Kirk turned to leave. "Well Bones, you've got nobody to blame but yourself."

The dilithium, Kirk mused as he strolled down the corridor, he could understand. As good as currency— no, better. A load of good crystals would be easy to market to some of the Federation's less reputable concerns. Or to any of many non-Federation worlds.

But why did they take the strobolin? Why? Pirates would hardly have known what it was. And if they had, they would have realized it wasn't particularly valuable—it was demand, not rarity, that was responsible for that.

Come to think of it, he considered as he entered the lift, that was probably it. They had taken the strobolin out of ignorance, reasoning that anything worth protecting so well was worth appropriating.

If only they had left the drug, he could have overlooked the assault, forgotten the injuries, ignored the monetary loss. Suddenly he grew cold as he realized that they might now have discovered the drug's true value and simply have destroyed it, or dumped it in space—out of anger, perhaps, for the valuables the security chamber had failed to yield.

He tried not to think about it, just as he tried to ignore McCoy's hypothesis about intership transfers of the stolen goods.

In one way the situation was made simple for him. Because of the restrictions imposed by time, he was reduced to only one course of action, spared the need of choosing among several tortuous possibles.

All they could do was follow the thread of radioactive residue and hope it led to the intact ampoules of strobolin. Hope it did so quickly.

Exiting onto the bridge he automatically scanned left to right, insured himself that everyone who belonged at his/her post was present. Arex, he noticed as he took his seat in the command chair, was back at the navigator's station.

Handling the dual assignment was hard on the Edoan, he knew. But he was a better backup to have there than anyone else in a situation like this. Sulu could cover for him where necessary.

Besides. he mused bitterly, one way or the other the navigator wouldn't have to occupy the dual position much longer.

"Report."

"Emanations from the radioactive matter still registering strongly on applied sensors, Captain," Sulu informed him. "Bearing still two hundred twelve plus, one hundred seventy-five minus. We are moving up on a massive grouping of solid material."

"Slow to standard cruising speed," Kirk ordered, fingers tap-tapping on an arm of the chair. "Free-space asteroidal belt or globe," he muttered to himself.

Sulu was busily replacing the abstract information listed on the main screen with a view from the ship's fore scanners. Such groupings, Kirk reflected, were not common, but neither were they rare enough to arouse unusual interest.

Visual sightings confirmed that this was a normal collage, jagged fragments ranging in size from microscopic pebbles to a few moon-sized specimens. At the moment, however, abstract analysis was far from his mind.

"The trail of radioactives enters the group and begins a weaving pattern, Captain," Sulu reported.

Kirk nodded slightly. He had half expected as much. They had been closing steadily on their quarry, judging by the upsurge in radioactive intensity of the trail. This was the closest thing to a hiding place open space offered to an interstellar craft.

"They're taking evasive action. A sensible maneuver, wouldn't you say, Mr. Sulu?"

"The ideal place to try and shake us, Captain," the helmsman agreed. "Especially if there are any natural concentrations of radioactives in this belt." He studied his port instrumentation.

"Preliminary indications point to many of the asteriods as having unusual energy properties that—" He stopped, staring at a particular readout.

"Share it with all of us, Mr. Sulu," Kirk said sharply.

"Extreme-range sensor scan indicates that the trail of radioactive debris we have been following ends in the approximate center of the grouping."

"Could be trying to cover their train somehow, trying to throw us off by running on a different drive system, or perhaps arranging some kind of unpleasant welcome," Kirk murmured, to no one in particular. "We can be sure of one thing, now—they know they're being pursued." He glanced back to Uhura. "All deflectors up—sound yellow alert, Lieutenant. Mr. Sulu, cut speed and maintain evasive approach pattern."

A chorused "Aye, sir" came back to him, while

bright flashes paired with suitably cacophonous whoops resounded throughout the starship.

"All sections secured and ready, Captain," Uhura was able to report minutes later.

"Thank you, Lieutenant. Approaching unknown's approximate sphere of confluence. Stand by for—"

A brilliant flare momentarily obliterated the scene depicted on the viewscreen, and the *Enterprise* shook to the force of destructive energies.

"What in the Pleiades was that?" Judging from the violence of the flare, alarm horns should have been sounding steadily.

Arex worked furiously to secure an answer. What he learned wasn't exactly encouraging, but neither did it appear they were under attack from some kind of unknown superweapon.

"Unusual energy properties indeed, Captain. It seems certain asteroids are composed of anti-matter. This entire belt is remarkable for having both matter and anti-matter existing side by side—a highly unstable configuration.

"Walking on a field of mined eggshells is more like it," Uhura suggested.

"All fragments explode on contact with each other—decidedly a dangerous place for a chase, Captain," the navigator finished.

"Their maneuverability's reduced, too, don't forget that," Kirk countered, scowling at the screen as if the universe were personally trying to make his life miserable. It was not a new sensation.

"Keep those deflectors on maximum, Mr. Scott." The chief engineer acknowledged the order from his place at the bridge engineering console.

"Captain? There's enough power locked in this belt to run whole fleets of starships. It would require a major industrial effort to tap it, but the amount of potential energy involved—"

"Enough to do a lot of damage, also, Mr. Scott. Steady and easy, Mr. Sulu, steady and easy." Sulu nodded.

They continued on through the belt, crawling impatiently along the still radiant, damning trail. Deeper and

deeper into the grouping they moved. Only the occasional flare of antagonistic elements obliterating each
other in inorganic suicide registered on the sensors.

Finally something else rocked the *Enterprise*. It was
a substantial jolt, but no one was thrown from his seat,
and Uhura was soon able to report all sections in with
no damage, no casualties.

This time the buffeting was caused not by
matter–anti-matter disintegration, but by a deep blue
beam which had struck at the *Enterprise* from just over
the horizon of a large asteroid below and to starboard.

"Mr. Sulu!"

"Fractional calibration completed, Captain. They're
running, but I've got them."

"Pursuit speed, Mr. Sulu. Phasers stand by."

It was only a matter of minutes, now. As they passed
he considered strategy.

Chances were their assailant had taken his best shot
first, hoping to disable the *Enterprise* before she could
retaliate. But the barrage they had taken wasn't anything on, say, the order of what a Klingon battle
cruiser could put out—though it could have messed
them up pretty badly if the deflectors had not been up.

On the other hand, the belligerent vessel's commander might be trying to draw the *Enterprise* into a
more tactically advantageous position for him. It was
too soon to judge. Best be ready for anything.

First round to the *Enterprise*, though—the attacker
had forfeited the element of surprise.

The starfield pinwheeled on the screen. One glowing
blob—blood red, unround, and of irregular outline—
was finally locked into its center.

"Hold them, Mr. Sulu." Another probing blue light
momentarily erased the view. "Analysis?"

Sulu was working smoothly, efficiently at the controls. "Standard frigate-class phasers, sir, slightly modi-
fied.

"Plenty hot enough to make scrap of an unarmed
freighter like the *Huron*. They'll never get through our
screens," Kirk noted with satisfaction.

"Captain," Arex broke in, "I've finally placed the
ship's markings. It's an Orion vessel."

"Orion," Kirk echoed thoughtfully. The Orions were an isolated, humanoid race who stuck close to their small system of three inhabited worlds and shunned contact with outsiders. There had never been any reason to suspect them of antagonism toward other peoples. They were simply thought to be naturally reclusive—until now, he mused furiously.

They were very human-like, but emphatically not interested in joining up with the Federation, with the Klingon Empire, or with anyone else. The corollary was that members of those and other multistellar political leagues expressed little interest in expanding relations with the Orions.

The perfect cover, Kirk reflected, for some wide-scale, unsuspected piracy. He found himself wondering how many ships had been pushed onto the missing-and-presumed-lost register at Starfleet HQ through the intervention of the *indifferent* Orions.

"They're hailing us, Captain," Uhura announced, just as he was about to order the first phaser burst.

"Put them through, Lieutenant."

Uhura made the necessary adjustments, and they were rewarded by the face of the Orion captain. It was accompanied by a harsh, defiant voice forming comprehensible words. It affected Kirk, who had been threatened by the commanders of full battle fleets, not in the least.

Had O'Shea or Fushi or Elijah been present, however, the first response to the alien's words would have been immediate and distinguished by its colorful invective.

"Enterprise," the Orion commander began, indicating that their detection instrumentation was working as well as their diffusion beam, "we demand you cease your pursuit immediately. As a representative of a recognized neutral government, I must protest."

Kirk controlled his anger with an effort. For the moment he had to try diplomacy. Besides, the Orion commander was technically correct.

"This is Captain James T. Kirk, commanding. Who said we were engaged in a pursuit?" The Orion didn't change expression. "We detected a malfunction in your phaser systems and thought you might require aid. You are experiencing a malfunction?" He grinned sardonically.

"No—but the way you crept up on us, we could not be certain your intentions were not hostile."

"I compliment you on your method of discovering whether or not they were," Kirk snapped back. "It leaves no room for idle speculation. As for your neutrality, Orion's position has been in dispute ever since the affair regarding the Cordian planets and the Babel Concordance of stardate ... well, I'm sure you're familiar with both date and circumstances.

"But it's a matter of more recent history that concerns me at the moment, Captain. Yesterday a Federation freighter, the *Huron*, was attacked in this quadrant, its cargo hijacked. As the first alien vessel encountered in the area, we request you to submit to search, as per Babel Resolution A twelve. Do you require time to consider your response?"

The Orion didn't go for the lead. A request for time would constitute an admission of guilt. Instead, the Orion managed a respectable smile.

"Orions are not thieves. I am sorrowed to hear of the hijacking of the Federation ship. We certainly hope you find the instigators of such villainy. As for ourselves, we hold no Federation cargo of any kind. And our papers permitting us to travel in this sector are quite in order. I must insist, Captain, that you end your hostilities toward us. If this harrassment does not cease instantly, we will lodge a formal protest with your government."

Kirk made a quick slashing motion, glanced back over his shoulder as the Orion's image vanished. "Tell him to stand by, Uhura."

"All right, sir." There was a brief pause, then she looked back at him. "They want to know why, sir."

"Tell them I have some internal bodily functions to attend to. If they want further details, supply them."

"Sir," Uhura responded readily.

"Mr. Sulu, anything yet?"

"A second, sir, I'm reconfirming." The helmsman had been working furiously at the project ever since they had made close contact with the Orions. He proved as good as his word, looked back to the command chair wearing a smug grin.

"Sensors confirm the presence of massive amounts of dilithium on board the alien ship, sir. It must be packed in their spare rooms and empty corridors. They're fairly bulging with it."

"What about the strobolin?" Kirk demanded.

Sulu's smile faded. "According to what I've been told, there was no reason for the drug to be shipped in large amount, sir. If they have it, it's too small a quantity to detect through their hull."

Kirk grunted. "All right. Reopen the channel, Lieutenant."

"Channel open, sir," Uhura replied as the puzzled face of the alien commander reappeared on the screen.

"*Enterprise* to Orion vessel, Kirk here," he began. He had made a mental note of how careful the Orion Captain had been in avoiding the mention of his name, those of any of his crew, or his ship.

"I have a proposal to make. If, by some miraculous chance, you *did* happen to encounter the *Huron* and if you decided—in the interests of common decency—to salvage its valuable cargo, and if by chance you overlooked the three—" his voice rose slightly "—critically injured personnel on board, you might also have obtained a small quantity of perishable drugs from a no doubt accidentally opened security chamber. We need those drugs rather desperately."

The Orion commander was manifestly not an idiot. Kirk could see the gears spinning in his opposite number's head while the silence lengthened. Finally, the other commander looked up and ventured softly, "What would this drug be worth to you—frivolously assuming we had experienced the totally unlikely series of circumstances you detailed?"

Kirk leaned forward, his fingers clenching tighter than he wished on the arms of the chair.

"You keep the dilithium shipment. No mention of the entire incident to Starfleet or in my log. Plus an additional standardweight container of dilithium as . . . ," he hesitated, grinned tightly, ". . . payment for the *salvaged* drug."

Another long silence while the Orion commander appeared to consider the offer. When he continued there was a hint of suspicion in his tone—understandable enough under the circumstances. But there was something else, an undefinable something Kirk detected which hinted almost of desperation.

Obviously he understood his strategic position. He had lost the element of surprise. He had lost the chance that the *Enterprise* might run afoul of an unexpected matter–anti-matter explosion.

Despite his natural instincts he probably found himself in a position where he would have to risk the deal.

"We keep the dilithium," he said finally, cautiously, "plus, our neutrality remains intact?"

Kirk nodded. A briefer pause this time, before the alien commander replied firmly, "We will consider your proposal."

"Very well. But make it fast. Kirk out." He immediately switched to intercom. "Kirk to Sick Bay."

"McCoy here," came the rapid reply.

"Bones . . . how much time?"

"Less than an hour, Jim. The strobolin'll be ninety percent-plus effective right up till the end—not much longer than an hour. His internal collapse is starting to snowball. There's not much I can do to slow it and damn little I can do to halt it. If I had one lousy ampoule—"

"Hold on a little longer, Bones, a little longer. We're close, very close, to getting it."

"The Orion is hailing us, sir," Uhura interrupted apologetically.

"I know you can do it, Bones."

"It's not up to me anymore, Jim," the filtered reply came back. "It's up to that abstract community of proteins we call Spock. Skill doesn't matter anymore—just chemistry."

"Kirk out." He swiveled. "All right, Lieutenant, I'll take the call now." He steeled himself for whatever answer the Orions might give.

"Your proposal is agreeable, Captain . . ."

Kirk slumped a little in his chair.

". . . with one qualification."

Kirk sat straight again, suddenly wary. "What kind of qualification?"

"Whether your people come for the drug or we transfer it to you involves the interchange of at most, minor personnel. Expendables." Kirk started to protest, but the Orion commander made a tired gesture requesting silence and Kirk forced himself to sit back quietly.

"No aspersions intended, Captain. But without assuming any real risk, you could obtain what you want and then turn on us."

"What," Kirk replied slowly, "would it take to convince you of our sincerity?"

"More persuasion than the universe possesses. However, we will settle for a face-to-face exchange, the drug for the container of dilithium. In the absence of available absolutes, risking one's own neck is considered the best substitute. I will meet you myself."

"Face to face." All kinds of danger signals were going off inside him. "Where?"

"An extremely large planetoid close by my ship. You doubtless have it on your screens. It has an atmosphere acceptable to both of us. We can predetermine the time and beam down simultaneously. I will hand you the drug personally.

"Your own presence will be most reassuring, Captain. Compared to it, the extra dilithium crystals are superfluous." A faint, nebulous hint of humor. "I believe we can do without them." He assumed a rigid, waiting posture. "Now it is your turn to consider."

"I'd . . . like to consult with my staff."

The alien made a sign of agreement.

"You'll receive an answer shortly. Kirk out."

VIII

"It's got to be some sort of trap, Jim." McCoy's fist slammed into the smooth wood of the briefing room table top in an uncharacteristically violent gesture.

"I don't buy this business of not trusting 'expendable' subordinates. I don't believe it anymore than I believe this space-pucky about your own presence being required on the exchange to satisfy some inexplicable alien sense of uneasiness. What's wrong with your giving personal assurance by communicator? I'll bet they've cooked up this whole scheme just to get a clean shot at you!"

Kirk's reply was noncommittal. "Maybe my presence is required for spiritual reasons, Bones. We don't know much about Orion culture, you know. Still," he added, forestalling another Aesculapian outburst, "I find myself agreeing with you."

"No doubt of it in my mind," Scott added from the far end of the table.

"Yeah. Sure." Kirk put both hands on the table, leaned forward intensely. "I could be a trap. But we've got no time to consider options, no time to devise means of devious subtlety to secure the strobolin.

"If we don't get our hands on it *fast*, Spock is going to die. Would he do less in a similar situation for any of us?"

McCoy was shaking his head sadly. "Why did you bother with this meeting, Jim. You had already made up your mind."

"Yes," Kirk confessed, "I had. But I wanted to see if either of you had another option to put forward—however hare-brained. Obviously, you don't."

"Oh, we're not going to do this without precautions—don't worry on that score. My communicator channel will be frozen open so that every word of what goes on will be broadcast on the bridge—even if it seems to the Orion Captain that I turned it off.

"Scotty, you'll be ready at the transporter, which will be locked on me at all times. At the first sign of anything underhanded, well . . . ," he stared at his chief engineer, "I'm trusting you."

"If this doesn't work, Jim," McCoy went on worriedly, "we could lose Spock *and* you."

"Nothing unique about the situation, Bones. Men have been going through similar ordeals since the dawn of civilization." He exchanged glances with each in turn. "Let's go to it, gentlemen, double or nothing."

The bridge of the Orion pirate was considerably smaller than its spacious counterpart on the *Enterprise.* Its complement was correspondingly reduced.

But the officers who manned its compact consoles and panels had more to worry about.

Everything had gone so well, her captain reflected, brooding in the command chair. The *Huron* had proven a rich prize, and they had ambushed her well out of communications range of any other ship. With no armament to speak of and a small crew, she had been an easy take.

Only this *gisjacheh* drug, this strobolin, had been intended not for delivery to some distant world, but for a free-space ship-to-ship transfer. To a ship already dangerously near. To a Federation battle cruiser, no less!

Now, despite his helmsman's best efforts to elude pursuit, the huge vessel had run him down and cornered him here. When he considered what would happen if news of the *Huron* attack ever reached diplomatic channels, he had made the inevitable decision. The only decision possible, really.

But to be sure first, as is the *bya-chee* bird before striking. He looked down to his executive officer.

"Status, Cophot?"

"We can't outgun the *Enterprise* and we can't outrun it, *Elt.* Nor can we penetrate her shields sufficiently to discourage her."

"No chance of escape?" he pressed.

"No, *Elt*, none."

The commander made his racial analog of a sigh, found no inspiration in a moment's meditation. "Orion's official neutrality comes before this ship, its crew—or its commander. There is too much at stake to take the word of one man—any man. He cannot give enough assurances that he will not at some time report the incident to Starfleet."

"No, sir," his exec admitted. "The only way to prevent that now is by achieving the destruction of the *Enterprise*. And the only way to do that," he hesitated in spite of himself, "is to destroy ourselves, too."

"Agreed. I had thought perhaps, an unexpected surge on our part, at the moment of exchange. Ram, overload their shields—"

"Your pardon, *Elt*," his first officer objected, "but there is a better way." He looked suddenly reluctant.

"Well, come on, out with all, Cophot."

"These asteroids," the other began, "contain among their number many which are anti-matter. Of those that are matter, many contain a high proportion of unstable radioactives. No danger to a man, they are concentrated in the planetary core, as in—"

"The one below us, that I'm scheduled to meet Captain Kirk on?" Understanding dawned.

"I have ascertained that this is so," the executive officer admitted. "Both ships will lay to hard by the planetoid. So close, if the core is triggered to reaction, both will be destroyed, despite the strongest defensive screens any ship could mount. The difficulty lies in the method of detonation. Mere phaser fire will not suffice."

"What then?"

"An adequately powerful explosive, which would provide the minimum number of high-energy particles. The material to make such a compact device has been providentially provided for us.

"Dilithium, yes," the commander agreed. "How could such a device be triggered?"

"I can manufacture a remote control which will—"

The captain's eyes brightened, and he waved his exec off.

"No, no. I've a better idea, Cophot. I'll do it by hand, carry the device down with me when I go to meet Kirk. I want the satisfaction of handing him his precious medicine and then seeing his face when I tell him he and his entire crew are going to the Dark Place with us. Besides, do not underestimate the detection equipment of this class of Federation cruiser. It could detect an old shoe beamed down to the surface, not to mention your proposed exterminator package."

"As you wish it, *Elt*," the science officer said admiringly. "I will commence work."

"Be certain, Cophot, you do a worthy job. It is not everyday one has the privilege of composing the mechanics of one's own destruction."

The first officer made a silent gesture of concurrence.

"A call coming in from the *Enterprise, Elt*," the voice of the communications master broke in. The Orion commander turned his attention from his first officer back to the viewscreen.

"What is your decision, Captain Kirk?"

"I accept your terms."

"Very well," the *elt* replied, keeping his tone carefully level. "We will provide suggested coordinates, or—" he performed the movements of indifference "—you may select them yourself. We will beam down in fifteen of your minutes."

Kirk stared at the screen, noticed McCoy's glum expression.

"What now, Bones?"

"I still don't like it, Jim, but as you said, we haven't got any more time. Spock . . ." He shook his head slowly.

The Orion commander spoke again. "Fifteen minutes or not at all, Captain Kirk."

"Yes, yes," Kirk replied absently. "Agreed. *Enterprise* out."

The screen blanked.

It was a world of compact extinction, where one could see the work of oblivion in small doses, and comprehend.

True, it possessed a breathable atmosphere, a thin

gaseous envelope through which jagged mountains rose against a deep purple curtain. Nothing crawled over its pockmarked surface. Nothing flew through its sad sky.

It was not an embryonic world, awaiting only the right combination of heat and water to give birth. Rather it was a king among cinders, a shard of some long gone larger globe which in itself had never seen life.

But now life appeared on its surface, in the form of two electrically hued pillars. There was nothing to observe this visitation save the constituents of the pillars themselves. The two commanders rematerialized barely a couple of meters apart.

Immediately the Orion captain noticed the tricorder Kirk held in one hand, while Kirk's gaze went first to the overlarge backpack slung over the Orion's shoulders.

Consideration of its purpose and contents were forgotten as his eyes were drawn down to the plastic cylinder the other held. It was filled with tiny cylinders, and they in turn were filled with the fluid that could give life to the dying Spock.

Most of the printing on the cylinder's label was too small to read at the distance he stood from it, but the name STROBOLIN stood out clearly above the archaic red-cross symbol. So that there would be no doubt, the Orion took several steps closer and held the container out to him for a better look.

"As promised, Captain, your serum. Scan it if you wish." He gestured at the tricorder.

McCoy had preset the sensors himself. Kirk pointed it at the translucent cylinder, pressed a switch. If the contents of the container were something cleverly designed to simulate strobolin, they would have to be the work of a master chemist. McCoy had gone over the 'corder's programing a dozen times.

The reading the intricate mechanism showed was clear, however. There wasn't a hint of molecular funny business. On the starship's bridge, everyone breathed a sigh of relief as the captain's voice sounded over the open communicator.

"Pure strobolin, Bones." He rolled the container of

dilithium over the smooth surface. It bumped to a halt against the Orion's legs.

"My half of the bargain. Want to check it?"

"No, Captain Kirk. I trust you."

"*Now* you trust me." Kirk shrugged. "However you please. I'll take that now and then we can both beam up." He reached for the cylinder.

The Orion commander skipped backwards a few steps.

"No, Captain Kirk, I'm afraid I can't permit that. You see, no matter how I strive to convince myself, I can't believe that word of this incident will not ultimately reach your superiors. If that happens, my world will lose its neutrality and be subject to Federation retaliation."

"Look," an exasperated Kirk began, "we've been through this already. If my solemn word is not good enough for you, you must know that you can't escape the *Enterprise*. We can follow you anywhere."

"Only if you have something to follow, Captain, and something left to do the following in, and someone to do it."

Kirk gaped at him and tried to unravel the riddle, not liking the way his thoughts were leading him.

On the bridge, Arex heard, and muttered, "I've been getting some unusual sensor readings, Mr. Scott. That planetoid's putting out a lot of noise and all kinds of radiation. But this is different—it's localized around the captain and the alien."

"What is it?"

"I'm not sure—it's not around them," he said excitedly, "it's in *with* them. There's dilithium down there with them."

"Of course," Scott noted. "The Captain took down with him, for the exchange, a—"

"No, no!" The Edoan's voice rose to an abnormal shrillness as his voice-box tried to catch up with his thoughts. "This is different. It appears to be barely stabilized!"

"You've been staring at my pack," the Orion commander was telling Kirk. "I don't wish to keep secrets. It's an explosive device. When triggered by me it will detonate the radioactive core of this planetoid. The resulting cataclysm will be considerable—quite sufficient to destroy your ship."

"Yours too," Kirk countered. He wasn't familiar with Orion culture, true, but somehow he was sure the expression that slid over the commander's face was his equivalent of a snide smugness.

"Why do you think my people have been able to maintain our operations for so long, so secretly and well, Captain Kirk? It is because all unsuccessful Orion missions end in suicide. When possible, we enjoy company."

"Mr. Scott," Arex half pleaded for a decision, a command, a call to perform—*some*thing.

"We can't warp out, because we'll lose the captain—and Mr. Spock," Scott thought out loud. He couldn't beam the Orion commander aboard because triggering the device on board would set off the dilithium in the ship's engines. The Orion commander . . ."

"The dilithium!" he shouted, battering at the intercom switch. "Transporter room—Scott here—dilithium crystals on the Orion commander, Kyle, pinpoint 'em and beam 'em up—*fast*!"

"An interesting experience, is it not, Captain?" the Orion was musing, his hand hovering over a switch set into his belt. "Often I've wondered what instant dissolution would feel like. Is there time to feel pain, to sense the coming apart of one's body? An intriguing question."

"Pinpointed, Mr. Scott," Kyle's voice resounded over the open speaker.

"Do it!"

Kyle shifted the proper instrumentation in rapid sequence, his eyes glued to one small dial.

"Ah, well," the Orion commander finished, "it is one thing to philosophize, but another to experience. I have made my peace—let us have reality."

He reached for his belt a second before Kirk leaped at him. Kirk grabbed both alien wrists—too late. The Orion's eyes clenched tight as he winced in anticipation, his finger breaking the trigger contact.

Another second and he found himself flat on the

ground. Eyes open again, he discovered to his horror he was still capable of discerning the stars overhead. They formed an irregular halo around the angry face of Kirk, staring down at him.

Kirk was able to relax his grip some, still keeping the Orion pinned to the ground. The alien commander was in shock. He offered little resistance.

"Reality, huh? I'll give you reality." He directed his words to the open communicator. "Scotty, energize."

That brought the Orion awake and kicking. He struggled to reach his own communicator. Kirk jammed a knee into the region of the other man's solar plexus, put pressure on both wrists. The alien slumped, grimacing in pain.

"I know it's not total dissolution," Kirk told him through clenched teeth, "but it's the best I can do—for now." He felt a twinge of vertigo, saw his vision start to fog. Soon the surface of the asteroid was bare of life once more.

Kirk's first sight on coming out of transport was of two burly security guards who stood covering the alcove from opposite angles, phasers drawn and ready. Then he looked back, saw Engineer Scott enter the transporter room. Scott made no attempt to conceal his relief.

The guards immediately took hold of the Orion and effectively immobolized him—though he was still too bewildered to offer much in the way of coherent resistance. While they checked him for weapons somewhat less lethal than planet-busters, Kirk was on his feet, rearranging his tunic and walking toward the waiting Scott.

"Captain," Scott began, emotionally drained, "that was too close. So close that—"

"Take your time, Mr. Scott, and think of something appropriate." He turned, approached the pinioned Orion and his guards. "I'll take that, Ensign," he said to one of the guards, taking the plasic container from his grip. "It's not a weapon."

He moved rapidly to the intercom, the precious cylinder of strobolin ampules now safely in hand. "Kirk to bridge—"

"Captain," Sulu's voice responded, "we heard—"

"Later, Mr. Sulu. Right now I suggest moving us several diameters out in case they decide to try that little trick again."

"Aye, sir!"

"Kirk out." He clicked off, looked back to Scott. "Let's get up to the bridge." Then a glance backward as he addressed the security people. "Bring him along, too." The five men started for the elevator.

"By the way, Scotty, where's the dilithium he packed?"

"Stabilized and on its way to the engine storage chambers, Captain, where it will be put to better use."

On board the Orion pirate, the battle on the bridge raged between confusion and desperation.

"I tell you they're both gone, sir!" the communications officer reported.

"Gone!" The science officer was incredulous.

"I was scanning as ordered, *Bhar*, when they vanished from the planetoid's surface—both the Earther and the *elt*. There was no warning, and sensors detect nothing like an explosion."

"If it didn't misfire," the exec thought furiously, "then they must have discovered the dilithium pack and disarmed it, somehow."

"*Bhar*, the *Enterprise* is moving. They are leaving the potential radius of destruction."

"Not only have they disarmed it, they know exactly what we intended. That also means that the *elt* has either been killed or captured." He hesitated. "We have one final choice. Contact engineering and tell them to arm the engines to self-destruct."

"We are going to try and ram, *Bhar*?" the communications officer asked questioningly. The first officer was too depressed to frame his reply in contempt.

Instead, he simply repeated what was already known. "They could lose us or destroy us on a whim. But if the *elt* has been killed, or performed *Vyun-pashan*, we still have a chance to preserve Orion's neutrality. To prove such a serious accusation they will need more proof than mere tapes can provide. We can at least deny them that."

"Open hailing frequency, Lieutenant," Kirk ordered as he emerged onto the bridge. He took up his position at the command chair while Scott moved to engineering

The Orion captain was positioned behind the chair where he could see the screen clearly over Kirk—and where he would be in clear range of the screen pickup. Kirk started to sit, noticed a subtle movement out of the corner of his eye. The Orion was moving his arm and hand upward, toward his mouth.

"Stop him."

Both guards reacted instinctively. Each grabbed one of the alien's arms, forced them up and back.

Kirk turned to eye the other closely. The Orion stared stonily at a point beyond Kirk's forehead.

"What are you doing?"

The Orion tried to sound bored. "My cheek itched, Captain. Does it startle you that I might try to scratch it? If you'll direct these idiots to let me go . . ."

"In a minute," Kirk answered absently. He looked downward, then knelt to pick up a small dark capsule. It was unmarked. He waved it under the other's mouth.

"Do I have to ask what this contains?"

Silence again.

"It *is* poison, isn't it?"

Still no reply. Kirk sighed, resumed his seat and dropped the deadly capsule into the chair-arm disposal unit.

"Commander," he said, carefully considering his words as he lectured the alien, "I'm sure your ship is preparing to destroy itself. Everything you've tried and said so far points to it as the logical course of action.

"If it does, your entire crew will have died for nothing. Because we're not going to let *you* commit suicide. Whether they live or die, you'll still stand trial. I'm sure both Federation officials and the representatives of other governments will be very interested in the results of the mind scans. I suspect it won't take very many to put a permanent end to Orion's little game of neutral piracy.

"Any reaction, Uhura?"

"I've finally raised them, sir."

Kirk nodded, peered back at his alien counterpart. The expression on that worthy's face was unreadable. Quite possibly it reflected similar emotions to those Kirk felt as he stared upward—hate, and respect.

To some races death meant little. Kirk didn't think it applied to the Orions. This man had meticulously planned his own destruction for the good of his people. Regardless of racial motivation, the key ingredient was still guts. Kirk had to admire them for that.

"They're acknowledging aural exchange only, Captain," Uhura reported.

"That'll do for now, Lieutenant." He spoke into the pickup. "This is Captain Kirk spreaking to the acting commander of the Orion vessel. We hold your commanding officer prisoner." He glanced back at the man in question, then continued.

"He is in excellent health and perfectly capable of communication—voluntary or otherwise. Rest assured he'll remain so." He stopped, spoke more softly to the silent figure behind him.

"Your choice again, sir."

The Orion captain made a resigned gesture with his head. Obviously he had already made up his mind. It confirmed Kirk's belief in the Orion's essential respect for life. He nodded to the security guards.

Both men let the alien go, but continued to watch him closely. Kirk leaned to one side and allowed the other a clear shot at the pickup.

"*Bhar* Cophot?"

Instantly visual contact was established, and Kirk saw the uncertain face of the Orion ship's executive officer staring anxiously back at him.

"*Elt*? Your orders?"

"Disarm the self-destruct system." Kirk noticed he didn't bother to ask if it had been engaged. The exec looked reluctant. "And prepare for formal surrender."

"Very well, *Elt*. Cophot out." The screen went dark—but not before the two aliens had exchanged a complex salute.

Something else impressed Kirk. Despite ample evidence of intricate preparation for self-immolation, both mental and physical, the first officer of the Orion pirate hadn't objected to the surrender order, hadn't argued, hadn't protested.

Having been presented with an unavoidable situation and having exhausted all preferable options, in the end they had elected to do that which would preserve life—much to Kirk's relief. There was hope for the Orions, it appeared.

Their moral foundation was sound—only the edifice itself was rotten. Once a few reforms had been introduced into their presently one-sided view of interstellar economics, they might prove to be good friends.

Kirk dictated the log entry as he strolled back toward Sick Bay. It was the kind of entry he enjoyed making.

"Captain's log, stardate 5527.4. The Orion privateer crew is in protective custody and their ship in tow. The *Enterprise* is back on course for Deneb five. We—"

No . . . no. He ended the entry. There were a host of details he could have added—but to what end? This was one entry that had intruded on an already hectic routine mission. A good place for brevity.

Their appearance at Deneb Five with an Orion vessel in tow would cause enough excitement. And Kirk had little use for fancy entrances. He much preferred a safe exit.

But it would eventually be good for the ship (the ship, the ship—always the ship). The fact that solving an unknown number of disappearances might gain him a promotion never crossed his mind—merely that it might enable them to get a few requisitions filled rather more quickly than Starfleet's sluggish bureaucracy usually managed.

The rewards of heroism, he mused as he turned a corner. Out of such odd things as the illness of one man do great things come.

Orion neutrality would be shown to be as solid as a shoji. The Klingons and Romulans would lose a potentially mischievous ally. And an enormous quadrant of uncertainty on the Federation's fringe would now be opened as safe for shipping, enabling escort vessels and personnel to be shifted to other tasks.

All because of a drug. He wondered how many times

in the past the history of whole nations could have been altered by the presence of an aspirin at the right place and time.

He heard the voices even before he entered Sick Bay. Glancing left as he entered, he saw Spock sitting up in bed and looking Vulcan for the first time since they had left Argo. Not atypically, he and the ship's chief medical officer were engaged in a raucous difference of opinion.

"There's no way you can deny it, Spock!" McCoy was shouting.

"I can deny it," Spock countered patiently, "by pointing out . . ."

McCoy cut him off, rambled—or rather rumbled, on. Sometimes Kirk wondered if they ever argued in complete sentences.

"I've waited a long time for this," McCoy was proclaiming loudly, as Kirk walked up to them, "and you're not going to cheat me out of it."

"Out of what?" Kirk inquired politely. Both Spock and McCoy temporarily turned their attention to him.

"Nothing, Captain. Dr. McCoy is endeavoring to gloat—a reprehensible condition characteristic of his unpredictable prehistoric leanings."

"Spock, that special blood of yours may have saved you a dozen times on other occasions, but this time it almost did you in. You can't deny it, now." The first officer leaned back in the bed and folded his arms.

"On the contrary, Doctor, I still have ample grounds for preferring my physiological structure to yours. As far as psychological structures are concerned, there is of course incontrovertibly no contest."

"I see, gentlemen," Kirk broke in, unable to suppress a smile, "that things are back to normal."

McCoy scowled. "Uh-huh—he's as stubborn as ever, Jim."

"Rational, Doctor," Spock corrected easily.

"Insane, Jim," McCoy shot back.

Sometimes I wonder if anyone on this ship is operating with undamaged circuitry, Kirk mused.

"I am surprised that you raise the question of sanity, Doctor," Spock went on, "as . . ."

Kirk gave up and walked away. He had had several questions he had wanted to put to Spock. Clearly they would have to wait until McCoy's peculiar brand of rehabilitation therapy concluded.

Meanwhile, at least he had the satisfaction of knowing that both patient and doctor were doing well, thank you. . . .

PART III

JIHAD

(Adapted from a script by Stephen Kandel)

IX

As things turned out, it was fortunate Spock's recovery was rapid. "Things" came in the form of a Class-A Security Prime Order—a classification so strict that Kirk was required to unscramble it himself, using a locked computer annex, in the sanctuary of his own cabin.

The instructions revealed by decoding were brief, even curt. They generated feelings of both puzzlement and anticipation in Kirk.

Something of both must have shown in his face as he handed Lieutenant Arex the slip of paper.

"Set course for arrival at these coordinates, Lieutenant."

"Very good, sir." The Edoan navigator took the slip, examined the figures inscribed thereon and commenced transferring them into the navigational computer. Only after he had completed the assigned task did he allow himself a moment of personal reflection.

When he eventually spoke, his statement was both fact and query.

"Captain, the indicated coordinates have been programed. We are proceeding toward them at standard cruising speed."

"Thank you, Mr. Arex." The navigator continued to eye him. "Was there something else?"

"Captain, I do not possess a perfect memory. However, there was something about our intended destination which prodded at me. Upon concluding programing, I checked out my supposition and found it confirmed.

"There is nothing of planetary size in the region we are headed for—much less at the specified coordinates."

If he expected Kirk to make a counterclaim or sup-

ply some new information, he was disappointed.
"You're quite right, Mr. Arex. That quadrant's as
empty as a spatial equator."

"A rendezvous, then, with another ship?" the navigator asked hopefully.

"At this point I'm not permitted to say, Lieutenant.
Although," and his voice dropped to a faint whisper
which Arex could barely pick up, "you might say
something like that."

Arex turned back to his console, more confused than
before. It might have consoled him to know that Kirk
was equally puzzled. Fearful of having made a mistake
in unscrambling, he'd gone through the decoding process three times. Three times he received the same reply from the bowels of the computer.

And each time the answer was just as enigmatic as
before.

Ordinarily he would have requested clarification of
orders so extreme from Starfleet. But Class-A Prime—
these orders were not to be questioned, only obeyed.
Such orders emanated only from the highest echelons
of Starfleet HQ. Something critical was up.

And yet, if it was so vital, why did the orders specify
they proceed at normal cruising speed? And what were
they expected to rendezvous with? Clearly, secrecy took
precedent over execution in this.

There was nothing cryptic about the instructions
themselves—only the rationale behind them. They
stated simply that the *Enterprise* was to proceed to
such and such coordinates, whereupon they would meet
something/someone at whose disposal they were to
place themselves.

That was all. No additional details or instructions.

It wasn't like Starfleet to supply such sketchy information to back an important order. So much hush-
hush suggested something else.

"Someone is badly frightened," Spock agreed.
McCoy had finally released him from Sick Bay, to the
great relief of both. But he could shed no further light
on the orders.

"There are no facts on which to speculate, Captain."

"Well then, Spock, we'll just have to wait until some-one supplies us with some."

There were surprises from the moment they neared the rendezvous coordinates, days later. An awful lot of people seemed to know about what purported to be an ultra-secret enterprise.

"I have *multiple* contact, sir," Sulu had reported, "at the coordinates—with something big at the center."

Hours passed. "Put what you can on the screen, Mr. Sulu."

The visual which resulted was revealing indeed. Numerous spacecraft were grouped loosely around the rendezvous point. They were as curious a collection of interstellar travelers as Kirk had seen in a long time.

At least half a dozen civilizations were represented here, possibly more. All were arranged—one couldn't quite say orbiting—around a huge green-and-silver ball. It radiated with the brightness of artificial atmospheric lighting. Against the total blackness of deep space and in the absence of a sun, it seemed to pulse gently.

Too small to be a planet, too small to be even a rogue moon. Too big to be a spacecraft.

In point of fact, it was all three.

Spock's gaze was riveted to the main viewscreen with an intensity rarely seen. "A Vedalan asteroid," he murmured. "I have never seen one before outside of bad pictures and worse sketches."

"Nor have I, Spock," admitted Kirk, likewise awed.

"Well I've even never heard of them, or it, or whatever you're talking about," Uhura broke in. "Somebody elucidate."

"The Vedala," Spock explained smoothly, "are the oldest space-traversing race known. They are so old that they long ago abandoned their worn-out home worlds to begin a nomadic life wandering among the stars.

"They travel at great speeds on large asteroids or small planetoids which have been remade to suit their environmental requirements. In addition to tremendous mobility, these tiny artificial worlds provide them with both personal and racial privacy—a quality they are known to value above all else.

"Yet for some reason, they now apparently require the presence of outsiders."

"And we're to place ourselves at their disposal," Kirk murmured, studying miniature mountain ranges, admiring the pocket oceans and manicured plains which studded the silver globe.

"Captain," reported Uhura, all business once more, "we're being scanned."

Kirk was reminded that the Vedala affected a pastoral veneer and took pains to avoid flaunting their technological knowhow.

What could they need the *Enterprise* for, then? Or these other ships, for that matter?

"Everybody sit tight," he ordered. Time passed as they drew nearer, then Uhura announced the replacement of the scanning signal with another.

"We're being hailed, Captain. No visual."

"Let's hear what we came to hear, Lieutenant." Uhura adjusted controls and an eerie, piping voice filled the bridge.

"Welcome, *Enterprise*. Welcome, Captain Kirk and First Officer Spock. We will expect you as soon as possible. Your coordinates for transporting down are . . ." and the voice ran off a series of figures which Uhura recorded, played through to the main transporter room.

"Please be kind enough to pardon the lack of visual welcome," the voice concluded, "but as you may know, we are extremely protective of our privacy. We regret any offense this may cause . . . but it is required."

"No offense taken," Kirk replied. "Coordinates received."

"Polite enigmas, aren't they?" Sulu commented.

Kirk was about to press further when an unobtrusive palm covered the armchair pickup.

"I think we had best meet politeness with politeness, Captain. Even asking the name of our greeter might be construed by the Vedala as an intrusion—even an offensive gesture."

"I think you're over-reacting, Spock, but . . . all

right." Deductions would wait until they finally met their hosts. He rose from the chair.

"Mr. Scott, you're in charge until Mr. Spock and I return."

"Very well, sir. Uh, might I ask, when might that be?"

"No idea, Scotty," he said, moving toward the door. He looked back at a sudden thought. "Why, Scotty, the Vedala have a reputation for paranoid secretiveness, sure. But they're not belligerent. Surely you're not worried about *them* doing us harm?"

"Not the Vedala, Captain, no—though I kinna trust 'em as completely as you seem to." He indicated the assembled starships circling the Vedala homeship. "But there're some ships out there that belong to folk who've been known to get nasty now and again. They could have representatives down there, too."

"I don't think the Vedala would let anyone run amuck on their homeship, Scotty, but don't worry. Mr. Spock and I will keep our communicators close at hand."

"Dinna worry—that's one order I never can seem to obey, Captain," Scott murmured—but Kirk and Spock were already in the elevator.

"Any idea what the specified coordinates will put us down on, Mr. Kyle?" Kirk asked the transporter chief.

"Something in the atmosphere seems to produce the daylight they receive on the surface, Captain," Kyle replied. "It makes direct visual observation very difficult."

"Consistent with what we know," Spock observed.

"*However,* the people down in cartography are fairly certain you'll be setting down on dry land, in a relatively level region."

Kirk and Spock assumed positions in the alcove.

"If you'll just take a half-step to the left, sir," Kyle requested. Kirk did so. Kyle manipulated several instruments at once, put his hand on the main switch. "Energizing, sir."

They stood in a grassy glade encircled by tall, lushly leaved trees. A small stream wound merrily down the low slope just before them.

But the sky overhead was strange. Kirk thought he detected a reflection from something solid. They stood under a transparent dome that sealed them off from the rest of the homeship. He could see where it curved down in the distance to meet the surface—undoubtedly to seal them in and avoid contaminating any more of the home than was required by common courtesy.

Yet, they had transported straight through it. Kirk didn't feel too confident about the accomplishment. Little enough existed in the way of Vedalan artifacts, but it was known that they were oustanding chemists.

Something that resembled an explosive was just as likely to be a composite made from vegetable shortenings, while a soap bubble might prove impervious to the strongest phaser. Yet any deceptiveness on the part of the Vedala was unintentional—or had been till now. It remained to be discovered whether that record would remain unblemished.

They could have made a great contribution to Federation civilization—or any Galactic civilization, for that matter. All entreaties to join or participate, however, were met with the excuse of painful shyness by rarely contacted representatives of the race.

It was the Vedalan way of refusing without insulting.

Besides, what could anyone offer them they did not already have or could not obtain on their own terms? For example, the presence of the *Enterprise* and various other vessels to carry out some as yet unknown task? But that was only common sense.

When the Vedala found it needful to call for help, it was in the best interest of all to respond.

Kirk couldn't tell whether the being standing before them now was the one who had addressed them on their approach or another. The Vedala was a small, furry creature, utterly inoffensive looking. It reminded Kirk of the pictures he had seen of the extinct aye-aye of Terran tropical forests.

Kirk looked around, found he was standing before a grassy knoll that formed a crude but comfortable-looking seat. Either Kyle had been inhumanly precise in his calculations or the Vedala had somehow seen to it they set down where they were wanted.

For the moment, Kirk's attention was wholly drawn to the representative of the ages-old race standing in front of them.

The Vedala made a gesture. Kirk blinked, stared. The grass around them was no longer flat and empty. Now he saw several other grassy knolls arranged in a semi-circle around the Vedala. They were occupied, and their occupants were neither human nor Vedala.

"Welcome, Captain James Kirk and Commander Scott," the Vedala intoned solemnly, turning Kirk's attention away from the other knolls. The creature spoke with a soft feminine contralto, which was at once reassuring and forceful. There was nothing fragile about it, and its strength belied the appearance of the toylike being who produced it. There was the power of millennia behind it. Kirk paid attention.

"I will introduce you to the others," the Vedala continued. It gestured first to a far knoll on which a winged humanoid rested, leathery wings fluttering uneasily against the too-near earth. The creature stood over two and a half meters high. Kirk recognized it from tridee tapes, though he had never met a representative of the Skorr before.

"This is Tchar," the Vedala told them, "Hereditary Prince of the Skorr, master of the Eyrie."

It was a measure of the strength of Tchar's character that Kirk and Spock paid any attention to him at all, considering the mountain that snuffled and grunted next to him. This butte of intelligent protoplasm the Vedala identified as one Sord. The reptile snorted a greeting. He very much resembled the bipedal dinosaurs who had dominated a long-dead piece of Earth's chaotic past.

But the forehead here was high, the forelimbs ending in hands with opposable thumb and fingers, the intelligence self-evident. Nor was Sord from a world like Earth. His body was bulkier than would be needed there, muscles on muscles the sign of a heavy-planet dweller.

The Vedala went on to the third member of the group, and for a moment Kirk and Spock failed to notice it, their eyes adjusted to creatures the size of Sord.

In direct contrast to its massive neighbor, it sat shivering on its grassy chair, trying to withdraw into the loam. Before the Vedala could proceed it interrupted, its voice thin and breathless.

Multiple cilia in place of upper limbs rippled nervously, goggle eyes darted from side to side in perpetual search for avenue of escape. "I was sentenced to this mad expedition," the asthenic ambassador announced, "I don't like it here. It's too quiet. I don't like any of you—no offense intended—I just wish I were back home in my city burrow."

"City cell is the correct appellation, I believe," the Vedala finally managed to say. "Em-three-green—an expert picklock and thief of extraordinary though peculiar talents, when he is not too terrified to demonstrate them.

"Em-three-green's people are . . . ," the Vedala hesitated ever so slightly, ". . . of an extremely cautious bent."

"We're cowards, you mean," corrected Em-three-green, not defiantly, of course—that would have been utterly out of character. "And I," he finished almost proudly, "am the biggest coward of all. I want to go home."

"Oh, shut up. I'm sick of your belly-aching!" broke in a disgusted, very human-sounding voice from the ciliated safecracker's right. Em-three-green uttered a sharp whimper, tried to bury himself even deeper into the grass.

"This," the Vedala continued, indicating a young female humanoid, "is Lara." She was clad in a tight-fitting, multi-pocketed one-piece tunic that covered her from neck to ankle.

"Lara is a huntress from a people who are natural hunters. She also possesses a unique talent—a flawless sense of direction which is as real to her as sight or hearing are to you. A necessary skill for where you are going."

"I was about to bring that up myself," Kirk replied. "We're going someplace, then? I was instructed only to place myself and my ship under your direction. We were told nothing more ... not even the fact that this expedition is to be multi-racial in makeup."

"Nor were any of these others," the Vedala informed him expansively. "This was done to preserve secrecy."

"You know as much now as we do," Lara added sharply. She looked toward the Vedala. "Who are these new ones?"

"Human and Vulcan," the Vedala informed her, with distressing matter-of-factness. "Mr. Spock was chosen for his analytical ability and overall scientific expertise. Captain Kirk, for his qualities of leadership and initiative, and a remarkably high survival quotient.

"There is, as you others know, one among you who knew by necessity the reason for bringing you here and the purpose to which your diverse abilities shall be put. Tchar will explain the mission, Captain Kirk, as he has to the others."

The Skorr rose, wings fluttering more violently. The words came out in a steady stream, in short, clipped phrases underlaid with controlled fury.

"Two or three centuries ago, humans, my people the Skorr were purely a warrior race. Our entire racial energies were bent to achieving one goal—a perfected militaristic society. This drive, coupled with our ability to reproduce rapidly, soon made us a threatening force in our sector of the galaxy.

"Today, we are a civilized people. Though we retain our military traditions and potential, we no longer live for war and destruction. All this has come about because of ... ," and he traced an abstract design in the air, his voice turning reverent, ". . . Alar."

"I know the name," Kirk recalled, nodding thoughtfully. "A religious leader with a reputation that extends beyond the Skorr."

"Our salvation and teacher," Tchar intoned solemnly. "He brought peace to us by showing how we might reconcile our violent desires with civilization, how we could direct our energies into constructive paths. He brought realization to the Skorr." Again he performed the peculiar, vaguely figure-eightish gesture.

"The complete brain patterns of this Alar," the Vedala explained, "were recorded by his apostles before his death and sealed in a flawless piece of sculpted indurite."

"And it has been stolen!" Tchar shrilled, wings flaring upward in anger. "Our soul, the soul of the Skorr peoples, has been taken from us!"

"To an outsider," the Vedala continued, "the effect of this theft on the Skorr verges on the inexplicable. The reaction has been extreme, violent, and uncontrolled. Thus, what this Alar was able to achieve in so short a time seems all the more remarkable.

"The Skorr have always been . . . ," the Vedala coughed delicately, "a paranoid race. Hence the havoc the disappearance of the *soul* has wrought among them. Exertions by others, most notably by the Vedala, for moderation in reaction have been ignored by the Skorr, whose latent belligerence has waited only for a cause to rise again to the fore. They now have that cause—though they would deny any desire to return to their ancient ways.

"Denials avail nought against the storm the theft has raised among them. Despite the fact that neither the thief nor the reason for the theft are known, the Skorr are preparing for war."

"But if the thief isn't known," Kirk objected, "who do they prepare against?"

"Since no Skorr could even conceive such blasphemy," Tchar informed him bitterly, "the abomination was clearly carried out by non-Skorr. That is whom my people prepare against. They will go to war with the rest of the known Galaxy and fight until they are no longer able to make war—or until there are none left to make war against. Unless—the soul is returned."

Shocked silence—eventually punctuated by a series of basso whoops from the bulky Sord. Lara the huntress smiled.

Kirk started to smile, too, until he noticed that not only wasn't Spock amused, he appeared unusually grim. He considered. The Vedala had made no move to counter what sounded on the surface like an outrageous claim—therefore, perhaps it might not be quite so outrageous.

After all, what *did* they know about the Skorr,

whose numerous worlds lay dozens of parsecs from the nearest Federation planet?

"It is a very real danger," Spock murmured. "Extrapolating from the most recently obtained figures, the existing Skorr population could breed an army of two hundred billion within a few years, with weapons technology to match. In the Skorr, fertility is tied to the aggressive instinct. The more anger generated, the more the population swells.

"According to the information supplied by Tchar and the Vedala, the Skorr now have the incentive to breed exponentially."

"But to fight the entire Galaxy—surely they couldn't win," the incredulous Lara objected.

"No, but what has that to do with it?" Tchar countered sadly. "You still fail to comprehend the mental state into which my people have been driven. Death now means nothing. Revenge, assuaging their anger—that has become all.

"No, my people could not win such a war, but what would that mean to the millions who would die, Skorr and non-Skorr? Fortunately, there are those among us who can still control their anger enough to realize what a jihad would mean to the Galaxy. But they can restrain the fury only so long, before they too are drowned in it and carried along by the madness.

"We *must* recover the soul before these final bastions of reason crumble!"

Kirk turned to the silent Vedala. "And there's no hint of who stole the soul?"

"None," the Vedala replied.

"It is hard to understand," Tchar told them. "What other race stands to profit from such a cataclysm? Yet to provoke such seems the only possible motive for the theft. Unless, of course, it was carried out by the mad."

"Insanity," the Vedala observed, "is possessed of and by its own motivations. The keys to unraveling such convoluted reasoning are merely less obvious. We have not been able to discover them."

The Vedala made its equivalent of a shrug.

"Someone, somewhere, may be furious beyond reason—at what, no one knows. Or the theft may be part of a grandiose suicide wish. None of this concerns us in the least. What does concern us very much is that such a war may hinder the free movement of the Vedala through space. Hence, we are involved."

"The Vedala," Kirk shot back, "are known to possess certain technological abilities beyond the combined talents of our Federation and other governments. Why don't you—"

The Vedala held up a restraining hand. "We prefer not to interfere directly. Also, there are indications that, were we to do so, whoever has stolen the soul would take steps to destroy it. We can direct, however, and suggest."

"All right," Kirk agreed. "If you can't take part openly, and you've no idea who engineered the theft, do you have any hints to the present location of the soul?"

Turning, the Vedala struck at empty air. At least, it looked empty. Whether the gesture somehow activated some invisible switch, Kirk couldn't tell. The Vedala were known to encourage confusion in others. It was a matter of protective coloration: what cannot be comprehended is difficult to coerce.

Whatever the method, the gesture resulted in the appearance of a large holographic projection. It drifted in mid-air in the center of the semicircle, just behind the Vedala. And as they watched, it moved and changed.

A star in space was all that was shown, at first. Then the star grew nearer, larger. Three planets were shown circling round it. Again they were drawn into the projection, which drew near to the middle world.

"The mad world," the Vedala announced, for the first time something like fear appearing amid that invulnerable calm. "See how it all writhes?"

Now they were plunging headlong toward the surface, now wheeling up to run parallel to it in a long, steady scan. A scan that revealed roiling, heaving plateaus; violently unstable crust; volcanos erupting, to be promptly enclouded by multiple cyclones; mountains upthrusting. Vortices of strange glowing gases suddenly appeared in a seemingly normal atmosphere, only to dissipate in minutes. Hail was supplanted by a rain of fiery ash.

"The recording you are seeing," the Vedala said quietly, "is being rebroadcast at normal speed."

Kirk whistled, leaned over to whisper to Spock. "And I thought the Terratin world was bad!"

Spock nodded agreement. "There are indications that the planet in question may be somewhat unsuitable for habitation."

Kirk muffled a reply as the Vedala spoke again.

"Seismically unstable, with radical seismic activity and unpredictable tremors. A most inimical climate. Severe tidal disturbances caused by the unceasing action of five moons possessed of the most perverse orbits—the list is endless, beings. The globe is a compendium of catastrophes. The temperature varies from twenty degrees Kelvin to two oh four above."

The Vedala made another gesture, causing the projection to shrink in size without disappearing completely. Kirk looked around the semicircle, saw with relief that here was something everyone present could agree on. All showed attitudes of respect.

"Somewhere on that world," the Vedala went on, "the soul of Alar is hidden." Again that odd hesitation, that hint of a crack in the pose of racial perfection.

"Three expeditions have so far attempted to locate and recover it. Three expeditions have so far disappeared. More care than before has gone into choosing the members of the fourth—yourselves.

"*If* you consent to participate. We will force no one."

The alternative, of course—Kirk smiled to himself. That threat was enough to persuade any rational being to want to help.

"Naturally, Mr. Spock and I will go," he said.

The Vedala looked gratified, offered no thanks, then looked around at the others. Sord grunted as though it made no difference to him one way or the other. Em-three-green might have declined, but was too thoroughly terrified to do more than shiver violently on his grassy knoll.

Lara acknowledged with a sharp whistle, while

Tchar's participation was apparently taken for granted.

"Seems we're agreed," Kirk observed.

"Then it is done," said the Vedala simply.

What happened then was in retrospect sufficiently impressive to outweigh any suspicion of obfuscatory technique. The Vedala began to glow, expanding, changing to a collage of misty particles.

At the same time the holograph enlarged. It swallowed the Vedala-mist, but didn't stop there. They were submerged in it. It flooded out the view of the garden around them. The sound of the little stream became a roar.

An unseen, unfelt torrent he could only hear washed over him and he felt himself falling, falling. Like being in a transporter operating somehow at a fifth normal speed—that was it.

Vision returned to him the same way, slowly, things coming into focus with painful patience. Globs of light and color gradually took on form and shape around him.

Minutes, and the globs had turned into rugged mountains, rain, vast glaciers filling narrow gorges, glowering storm clouds. The dull drone in his ears split into winds buffeting his body, the patter of raindrops on naked stone, and the violent hissing of volcanic ash and lava meeting an advancing river of ice. Kirk was stunned to see that the glacier advanced fast enough that the movement could actually be seen.

He turned slowly.

They had been set down on a broad, flat rock of immense size, utterly devoid of any growth whatsoever. Mountains towered on three sides. Bracing himself, Kirk leaned into the wind. Presumably this was the stablest place the Vedala could find to set them down at. Until he saw the cart, he wondered if the Vedala expected them to find and recover the soul with bare hands and intuition.

The crude-looking wheeled vehicle seemed hardly to represent the zenith of Vedalan technology. But closer study revealed it was designed with typical Vedala cunning. Most of its capabilities were concealed behind the awkward-looking exterior.

To fool any potential attackers, undoubtedly.

Kirk recognized the basic design of the compact drive system. It would drive the cart up anything other than a vertical face. The suspension system was of matching sophistication. Kirk hoped the on-board equipment had been prepared with equal thoughtfulness.

A shrill cry came down to him from above. Leaning back, he saw that Tchar was now in his element—whirling, diving, coming down finally to hover just above them.

"I cannot feel the soul!" he screamed angrily. "It is nowhere near. We have been tricked!"

"I think not," Spock disagreed, raising his voice only enough to rise above the smothering susurration of the wind. "Consider that the surface of this planet is in constant flux. The Vedala warned us of this. I would guess they have provided us with some means of determining the proper direction."

Kirk had already mounted the cart and was examining the protected instruments. There were plenty, and it took him time to sort out the various controls. They had been designed for use by creatures with all kinds of different manipulative members. But the drive controls were not what finally drew a smile from him, but rather the very instrumentation Spock had suggested they would find.

Kirk became aware of motion beside him, saw that Em-three-green stood there, staring under his arm. Finding himself detected, the little alien hastily moved away on the pretext of studying other controls. Apparently he found any close scrutiny threatening.

Kirk moved to the railing, saw that Sord and Lara had joined the argument.

"All right, save your breath, friends. There's directional equipment on board and it's already tuned. Guess what it's been tuned to?"

"Refined indurite," Spock said without hesitation.

"Exactly."

"Then why not tell us that before, instead of riskin' anything like dissension?" Lara wondered.

"The Vedala," Kirk explained, "probably don't want

to take any chance on our starting out overconfident. Putting us down here mentally naked was putting us down alert."

"Small worry of overconfidence," Em-three-green grumbled from behind him. "I can operate this machine, Captain Kirk."

"That's all right, Em," Kirk told him. "I'll manage it."

"No, let me, Captain," the little safecracker protested, with a rare show of determination. "I will feel useful, we will get where we are going faster, and," he added softly, "it will help keep my mind off this spine-lined burrow of a world."

Kirk nodded, watched as Em-three-green clambered into the control seat and touched controls with deft assurance. Instantly, a smooth rumble sounded beneath them, rose to a roar of power before settling down to a steady hum.

Spock climbed aboard, moved to examine the directional instrumentation. Kirk bent to give Lara a hand up. Grinning, she made a startling leap, grabbed the railing with both hands and pulled herself up.

That left only Sord. Kirk eyed him uncertainly and was rewarded by a bellowing laugh.

"There's room for you in the back, Sord."

"No," he boomed, "you little ones ride if you wish." The shovel-like head moved like a crane to take in the landscape. "I like this place—it's got variety. And I would crowd you."

Kirk studied the glacier, fascinated. Now it appeared to be retreating visibly.

"Captain," Spock called.

Kirk walked over, his attention going immediately to the small glowing screen the first officer was working with. A grid lay over the lit rectangle, beneath which a web of flexible lines weaved and pulsed. Abruptly they shrunk to a single, pulsing dot.

"It would seem our direction is clearly indicated," Spock observed.

Even as he spoke, the carefully aligned grid suddenly shifted, the dot expanding into a loose maze of questing

lines racing crazily across the screen. A red glow began
to suffuse the clear plexalloy.

"The position is shifting," Spock commented, "I
think ..."

Em-three-green leaned over from the pilot's chair.
When he got a look at the screen, his already wide eyes
bulged enormously.

"Shifting—the control elements are unphasing!" As
the solid lines of the grid began to break up, Em
screamed and jumped out of the chair to dive behind
the metallic bulk of the engine.

A whistling sound began, rose rapidly in volume.
Small whisps of smoke appeared from behind the
screen's upper corners. The whistle began to pulse
alarmingly.

Spock glanced at Kirk, whereupon both men dropped
to the deck. Thus they were missed by the flying
shards of acrylic and metal which screamed by overhead as the screen blew up.

Getting to their feet slowly, they grimly eyed the
smoking, sparking ruin that had been their one hope
for tracking down the soul. "What did the Vedala call
it?" Kirk muttered tightly. "The mad planet?" He gestured disgustedly at the ruined instrumentation.

"How do you explain that, Spock?"

"A confluence of unbenign electronic forces," the
first officer responded slowly.

"In other words, you don't know?"

"Precisely," Spock confessed.

"Doesn't matter."

Kirk turned, stared at Lara. She grinned.

"I know the way," she said. "I got a good look at
that thing before it went mockers." She turned, cocked
her head slightly without losing the grin and nodded in
a direction slightly to the southwest. Her voice was
matter-of-fact, confident. "That way."

A querulous inquiry drifted down from above: "Are
you certain, human?" questioned a hovering Tchar.

"For sureness, birdman," Lara threw back. "I can't
be fooled about directions and I can't get lost. That's
why I'm here." She pointed again, downslope and out

of the mountains. "It's that way, or I'll eat my kill-boots."

"The Vedala would not have chosen Lara had her abilities been less than perfect," Spock commented.

"So then," Kirk observed, "we know which way we're supposed to go—but we're meant to travel on the ground. An overview could be very helpful." He glanced upward significantly.

Tchar's wings spread wide and he beat downward to gain altitude. "I will scout ahead," he replied simply. Beginning a wide circle that brought him into the up-drafts sweeping up the granite flanks close by, he soared effortlessly higher.

Spock studied his progress for a long moment, then looked idly over at Kirk. "I will acquaint myself with our supplies." He moved toward the rear of the cart and the metal cabinets bolted to the deck there.

Lara watched him go, moved a step nearer Kirk. "Vulcans," she muttered. "Never liked 'em much myself. Cold-blooded critters, every one of 'em. Not an ounce of real feelin' in the whole pack."

"I wouldn't be quite so harsh," Kirk objected. "Especially on Mr. Spock. He's something of a unique personality."

"But not human, like you and me," she said huskily, eyeing him boldly.

Kirk said nothing, stared back in disapproval. She wasn't intimidated.

"Look, maybe you got different customs where you come from, Captain. My world, there's a lot of women, not so many men. When we find a man attractive, we say so." If anything, her gaze grew even less inhibited. "I'm sayin' so. How do you find me?"

"Fascinating and not a little overwhelming," he replied, responding to the frontal assault with complete honesty. "The only problem is, we're not here on a pleasure trip."

"All the more reason to take whatever pleasure there might be in it." She laughed, brushed teasingly close and walked to stand at the front of the cart.

Kirk studied her progress, the supple form and smooth stride. A host of alternating images melted together in his mind to form a single, highly confusing whole.

The muted hum rose in volume as Em-three-green got the cart moving. It lurched down the gentle slope in the direction Lara had indicated. Sord loped along just ahead, his movements cumbersome, awkward—irresistible.

"I've checked out the supplies, Captain."

"Hmmm—what?" Kirk mumbled absently.

"The supplies, Captain, I have completed an inventory," Spock repeated, slightly more forcefully. Kirk finally turned his attention to his first officer. Spock made a show of clearing his throat, continued.

"As expected, the life-support material is more than adequate. There are specific provisions for Sord, Tchar, and Em-three-green. And—there are weapons."

"Against what would we need weapons?" Kirk mused. "I thought the only hostility we were expected to encounter arose out of the planet itself? There's not supposed to be any native life here—unless the Vedala plan another surprise for us."

"I would not rule out anything at this stage, Captain. Judging from the Vedala's outspoken aversion to this world, it would not surprise me to discover that their preliminary survey of it was less than all-inclusive. We have the evidence of three previously unsuccessful expeditions to back this." He scanned the overcast, threatening landscape pessimistically.

"Nor are they, by their own admission, omnipotent. We must rely on our own abilities, I think. Overmuch reliance on Vedalan intervention may have doomed our predecessors here." He nodded toward the horizon.

"To steal something like the soul of Alar and then depend wholly on mechanicals to safeguard it strikes me as unworthy of any beings capable of devising such a theft in the first place. Also illogical. I suspect that before we regain possession of the soul, we may have to deal with those immoral beings personally."

Kirk murmured agreement and turned to contemplate the terrain ahead. Spock had only recited the obvious, yet it seemed as if the pulverized stone that crunched steadily beneath the wheels of the cart now whispered imperceptible threats at every turn of an axle, and unknown forms of extinction paced them while staying just out of sight.

In all this world, he sensed not a hint of welcome. He would be glad when they left it.

Or if . . .

X

Eventually the slope leveled out and the mountains sank beneath the horizon behind. Gravel and rock gave way to a broad, flat, desertlike plain of sand and fine, soft stone. Only scattered monoliths of black basalt broke the gently rolling plateau, volcanic plugs—the mummified hearts of long-eroded fire-spitters. Fortunately the cloud-laden sky cut much of the daytime heat, or they would have been broiled quite thoroughly. In fact, a brisk breeze had sprung up and now blew coolingly in their faces.

A short, violent chuff brought them to a halt. Sord snorted again and pointed ahead with a finger the size of a man's thigh.

"Now what could that be?" Everyone stared into the distance.

Moving in their direction was what looked like a solid curtain of dark gray. The breeze freshened and beat at them with increasing intensity. Kirk glanced questioningly at their furry driver.

"Em, is there a top to this thing?"

"I don't know," the little alien replied fearfully. He started hunting among as yet unused controls.

"I think so . . . no, that's not it . . . nor that . . ." The gray wall had moved nearer and was now charging down upon them.

"If there is, you'd better find it fast," Kirk warned. He yelled ahead. "I hope when you said you liked variety, you mean a broad definition of the word, Sord." The huge reptile did not reply. He was staring at the approaching wall.

The deluge reached them moments later, a rain of seeming solid intensity. Kirk had experienced a downpour like this only once before, on a deceptive world in the Taurean system. He and Spock had heen in the jug there, too.

Em-three-green finally unraveled the mystery sequence involved and got the translucent canopy up, just before they would have been washed away.

Lara wrung water from her hair, smiled radiantly beneath the damp strands. "*Real* weather."

"And a half," Kirk agreed readily, looking out through one of the clear ports. "You'd almost think—"

Before he could finish the thought, the rain stopped —as abruptly as a curse, to be replaced by a blaze of sunlight. Clouds began to form immediately, but under the attack of the sudden inferno, broad shallow lakes disappeared before their eyes, hissing, all but boiling off the sand.

Where vision had been obscured seconds earlier by a solid wall of water, now the landscape shivered and rippled under agonizing heat. Distortion waves added ridges and hills to the desert where none existed. And the distortions were suddenly multiplied as a faint quake shook the cart.

"We'll all die here!" Em-three-green wailed as he put down the canopy. Every one of his many cilia were locked to a control or structural segment of the cart.

"A statistical probability," was Spock's uninspiring comment. Lara eyed him disgustedly.

"Don't you ever act on anything besides your precious statistics, Vulcan?"

"Yes, but philosophy does not appear to be an adequate vehicle on which to base a course of action here," he replied unperturbed. "Nor do I find reliance on instinct satisfactory, as you seem to."

"Oh well," she shrugged, "to each his own."

Further discussion was interrupted by a shrill keening from above. A faint spot appeared, resolved into a slim, limber body centered between a pair of batwings—Tchar. Kirk wondered for a second how the birdman had survived the fury of the momentary monsoon, then realized he must have climbed above it.

"I can see something far ahead," he shouted down to them, "it's . . . ," and his last words faded into inaudibility as he banked and glided down to land atop the next rise.

Em-three-green swung the cart neatly against the base of the low hill Tchar had perched on. It was a short climb for the rest of them.

The object which had excited Tchar's concern was far enough away to be little more than a hazy outline. It was impressive nonetheless.

A simple cube of some black material, the structure sat utterly alone at the bottom of the vast sink. A sense of its enormity penetrated all the way to the valley's rim—though Kirk couldn't be certain just how large it was. The object was still too far away to judge accurately.

It also, he noted, lay exactly along the line Lara had indicated.

Tchar was fluttering, hopping about on the sand nervously. "I sense it, I can feel it—the soul of Alar is down there!"

A gigantic rumble shook the earth behind them, and the ground shivered in pain. Lara whirled, shouted something in shock that was drowned by Em-three-green's screams and Sord's locomotive whistle.

With absolutely no warning, a fountain of black ash and smoke had exploded from the ground. Like a film running at thrice normal speed, the crevice widened, expanded: then a half-formed volcano erupted skyward. In seconds, it was a hundred meters high and growing with incredible speed.

A crack appeared in the southwest cliff of the cinder cone. A stream, then a river of syrupy red-orange lava poured from the flank eruption. It rushed toward them like a wave of red-hot sand. The pressure below, Kirk knew, must have been enormous to produce such a voluminous flow in so short a time.

They hardly had enough time to realize how precarious their present position was. They sat on a slight rise, but one that was still well below the level of the cinder cone. It would wash this tiny summit clean before the flow subsided.

"It seems that everything happens with remarkable

speed on this world," Spock observed. "We may expect volcanic action at any time."

"I can see that, Mr. Spock. Question is, how do we go on remaining observers?"

"The Vedala made you the nominal leader here, Kirk," Lara admonished him. "*You* think of a way out."

"We have several minutes before the flow reaches us," Spock commented easily. "Plenty of time."

Not enough, it seemed, for Em-three-green. Whether it was the molten death racing toward them or Spock's seeming indifference toward it no one knew, but the little alien let out a pitiful screech and dashed down the slope to cower between the huge wheels of the cart.

Lara eyed Spock as if he were personally responsible for the approaching disaster, then she loped down to try and comfort Em. Sord huffed once, sat down on the sand and engaged in some steady nonverbalization of his own.

"I must point out, Captain," Spock went on, "that the vehicle we have been provided with lacks sufficient speed to escape so rapid a flow." He peered into the distance. "I also estimate that the flow is too wide for us to outflank."

"Not entirely true, Spock. We can still outrun it—if we let the engine draw maximum, unhindered power. I know this type. There's enough energy there to run circles around that flow."

"One high speed might be possible," Spock conceded. "But the power leads must be rerun, certain safeguards removed, emergency insulation installed. The total readjustment is complex and time consuming."

"Can't you handle it, Spock?" The first officer hesitated, finally shook his head.

"I know what is involved, Captain, but I have not the skill to perform so complex and complete an operation in so short a—"

"Excuse me for interrupting." They both turned, looked down to see the still shaking form of Em-three-green staring up at them. "I have some skill at digital manipulation. I can do it in time, I think, if," he gazed evenly at Spock, "you can direct me as fast as I can work, sir."

"Still not enough time," Spock insisted.

"We might be able to divert the lava flow temporarily, Spock," Kirk suggested. They had started down toward the cart. Em-three-green was already laying out the tools he would require. He glanced back over his shoulder. "Tchar, see if there's a suitable place."

The Skorr shrilled acknowledgment and launched himself into the pumice-darkened sky.

"Such a diversion would be at best of short duration, Captain, unless the flow of molten rock lessens significantly. It shows no sign of doing so."

"You worry about reprograming the cart engine, Spock, and let me worry about the lava."

They stared at each other a long moment, then Spock nodded. "Quickly then," he yelled to Em-three-green. Kirk noticed that he didn't bother to question the alien's abilities. Em-three-green had better be able to do what he claimed, and that was all there was to it.

Spock had the protective panel over the engine housing off in seconds. A moment sufficed to satisfy him as to its contents.

"This is Federation equipment," he told the tool-laden Em-three-green, "can you . . . ?"

"Anything anyone put together I can take apart," the little alien piped firmly. "We're wasting time."

Spock simply nodded, began: "Terminal M-three red leads to diode channel twenty-seven, cross-connects to CCa-fourteen . . . taking care not to break the fluid-state sealed component Three-R . . ."

Em-three-green's cilia were a blur. Spock experimentally stepped up the pace and the little alien kept pace easily, rearranging and realigning the critical instrumentation as fast as Spock could recite instructions.

Spock was willing to concede as how they now had an outside chance at survival—but still outside!

"Capain Kirk!" Kirk looked upward, away from the work in progress on the cart, to see Tchar hovering overhead.

"There is a ravine," the flyer shouted, "sixty meters

to your left." Kirk stared in the indicated direction and spotted the slight break in the ridge between them and the volcano, which roared on unabated.

"I see it."

"If it can be blocked," Tchar said, even as Kirk came to the same conclusion, "the lava will flow past and have to top the ridge to reach us. It will save some time."

"Good enough." He turned. "Sord?"

"I heard him," the organic mountain grumbled. Elephantine legs working smoothly, he lifted himself from the sand and lumbered off toward the ravine. Kirk and Lara followed as fast as they could, Lara politely slowing to keep pace with the slower Kirk.

"Carefully, Em-three-green," Spock warned, perceiving what he thought to be a just-missed movement on the part of the alien that would have caused a fatal short. One improper connection, one mixing of supercooled fluids, one wrong touch of an instrument on a live component, and the cart could go up in pieces—along with its present pair of occupants.

"I know, I know," Em-three-green muttered softly. "I'm trying to be as careful as possible at this speed. Please try not to make me nervous."

Spock returned to the dull, steady drone of instructions. He forebore to mention that Em-three-green's impossibly rapid, seemingly haphazard style of making the most delicate adjustments was making him not a little uneasy himself.

Sord was containing his impatience with difficulty by the time Lara and a wheezing, puffing Kirk finally arrived at the far end of the ravine.

Lara didn't bother to rest; instead she scrambled spiderlike up a sheer cliff. She looked toward the volcano, then back down at them and made hurrying gestures.

Kirk took out his phaser. Adjusting it for tight-beam, high-intensity work, he began slicing huge chunks of rock from the opposing cliff face. He was cutting at another piece before the first gigantic slab of sandstone crashed to the ground.

Sord put his sternum against the boulder, slipped

both hands around and under, and shoved. By the time Kirk had another block cut from the ravine wall, the huge reptile had the first one set in place.

Cut and place, place and cut, while Lara shouted constantly at them to hurry.

The mouth of the arroyo was finally sealed, faster than Kirk would have believed possible. He hadn't counted on Sord's incredible strength and endurance. They still had some time, so he busied himself cutting smaller fragments. Sord used them to chink small gaps in the main boulders.

They stopped only when Lara's anxious cry of "Here it comes, get out!" reached them.

As Kirk turned and ran, he could hear the nearing hiss from the lava as it sizzled over the sand. He glanced backward, like Lot's wife—and fell.

A moment later the sand was rushing past beneath him. Sord had scooped him up and was carrying him easily in both hands. Behind them the hiss rose to a furious, tense, spitting sound. Sord reached the end of the ravine and felt confident enough to turn and stare.

Jets of molten stone squirted between the uncaulked chinks in the makeshift dam. The topmost boulder seemed to quiver a little at the impact and slide backward slightly. But it didn't fall.

Lara pulled up next to them, panting from the run. She looked from Kirk back to the dam.

"Workin' real nice. For a minute there I wasn't sure it was goin' to hold. The flow's spreading sideways now, though. The lava in the cracks is cooling fast, cementing the whole job."

"How soon before the flow reaches the ridge-top?" he asked.

"Soon enough—but it doesn't matter. I've got our escape route."

"It better be a direct one." He gestured back toward the dam. Sparks were already dancing above it. They had a few extra minutes at most before the lava reached it and flowed down toward them once more.

A shout behind them. They turned in time to see the huge cart send up a shower of sand as Em-three-green swung it to a stop.

"The drive has been reprogramed—expertly," Spock announced. "Quickly, Captain. I do not know how long it will last."

They raced for the ladder as Tchar swooped low, spiraled overhead. Kirk hustled aboard, with Lara right behind. A rumbling query sounded behind him.

"Captain, I'm afraid that while I'm near to being invulnerable, I am not immune to the effects of molten rock. I fear I must crowd you temporarily."

"Get aboard, Sord," Kirk told him. "We'll manage." He and Lara moved to the front of the cart. Spock joined them there, leaving only Em-three-green near the back, at the drive controls.

Moving as quickly as possible but with infinite care, the great reptile struggled onto the rear of the cart. Even so, he nearly overturned it in the process.

"Careful, you monstrous scaly lump!" Em-three-green squeaked—out of fear, of course, not boldness.

"Move this machine, insect-eater," Sord countered disdainfully.

"Twenty-one degrees east," Lara ordered, pointing, "to take us out of the flow path. Then we can circle around and back toward the cube. I don't think—"

A titanic explosion shook the ground, nearly knocking everyone to the deck. Kirk looked behind them, was startled to see that a secondary cone had joined the first and was pouring out lava at a rate equal to its neighbor. The flow had suddenly doubled.

By tomorrow the abrupt action of wind, flood, and quake would probably have wiped out all signs of the entire eruption, he mused. They didn't have time to wait around and witness it. They didn't have even minutes.

The new eruption sent a shower of glowing sparks raining down on them. The engine roared, coughed, roared, coughed.

They weren't moving.

"Something is wrong!" Em-three-green shrieked, nearly losing his voice from panic. Behind them, a red-orange wave from the second cone surged against the ridge-top—flowed over and downhill. The added influx of fresh material was too much for the hastily erected dam. It collapsed. A stream of lava, topped with broken black crust, raced out and headed toward them.

"Quickly, quickly!" Tchar shouted down at them. "What's wrong?"

"I do not know." Em-three-green frantically studied gauge upon gauge, tried two dozen switches. "Something has caused the front shaft to lock. It must be—"

Spock was already over the side and ducking underneath the cart, tools in hand. Kirk raced to the railing, leaned over. Spock was out of sight.

"Spock?"

"One moment, Captain." A hysterical pause, then, "I have it. Sand has entered the mechanism through a broken lubrication seal. I'm cleaning it out and taping it, but it will clog again."

"Forget it, Spock, the power plant will have burned itself out by then." He looked to the ridge. The lava would reach them in three, maybe two minutes. "For Vulcan's sake, get back aboard!"

"A second, Captain. There, completed." Spock came into view, his hands and face smeared with some blue-tinted grease. At the same time, the first volcano regurgitated a plug of plutonic phlegm. A storm of fiery sparks and small globs of lava hailed down on them.

Kirk tried to cover up, as did everyone else. The bombardment passed quickly. He looked over the side again.

"Spock—Spock!"

The first officer was sprawled on the ground like a broken doll. One hand fluttered feebly at his head.

Kirk didn't think. Both hands on the cart rail, he vaulted over the side and landed with a jar on the sand. He rolled Spock onto his back.

"Leave," he muttered painfully, "all of you ... go."

"Not without you," Kirk objected.

"Captain, I ..."

Kirk got a shoulder under an arm, lifted Spock to his feet. "No, Sord, stay aboard. It'll take too long for you to get back on." Kirk staggered toward the ladder.

"Tell Captain ... ," Spock was mumbling, "... get others away."

"We're *all* getting away," Kirk whispered. Another explosion sent fire down on them. The odor of sulfur had grown nauseating. This time, no one was hit except Sord, who simply brushed the sizzling embers off his hide. Lava bombs the size of the one that had struck Spock he didn't even feel.

Em-three-green was gesturing hysterically at the approaching river of flame, screaming. Even Lara's reserve seemed ready to crack. Sord eyed the flow, then leaned over slowly. The cart creaked, supports and axles groaned. The wheels on the cart's opposite side rose off the sand. Em-three-green was too terrified to scream as the vehicle tilted precariously.

A massive paw grabbed Spock around the waist and lifted him onto the cart.

"*Go!*" Kirk screamed, clinging to the ladder.

Fear lent even more speed to Em-three-green's incredible reaction time. A roar of power drowned out even the sound of the closing lava as the cart's engine, rigged to permit it to pull energy unrestrainedly from the power pack, cut loose.

Kirk felt himself wrenched backward, locked arms and legs around the ladder and prayed the metal would last as long as his muscles. The front of the cart rose into the air from the force of the blast as it shot forward at an incredible turn of speed. Em-three-green adjusted controls, all four wheels hit the sand, and it shot down the slope seconds before an advancing cliff of red covered the spot where they had been.

Lava boiled angrily behind them, orange talons reaching after. But the flow was receding rapidly into the distance. Drive whining madly, wheels and axles spinning at a rate for which they had not been designed, the wagon raced away from the burning crest behind. Sparks were starting to fly from anguished components.

Tchar watched as the cart below reached the gap in the slope Lara had indicated. It raced through, over another slope and down a winding ravine, narrowly scraping stone walls and abutments. Here the downward slope of the land lay to the south instead of toward the black cube. The lava river would slam up against the ridge they had just raced over and turn harmlessly to the left.

At the end of this pleasant thought, there was a violent, grinding wail from the engine, mirrored by one from Em-three-green. He shut everything down with incredible speed, still not fast enough to reduce the shower of sparks now spitting from more and more sections of the car.

"Off, off, off, everyone off!" the little alien cried, even as he was running for the ladder. Flames began to belch from sealed innards.

With Sord carrying the still dazed Spock, they hurriedly abandoned the smoking cart. Taking shelter behind the first rank of sand dunes, Kirk turned, could make out a thin line of red orange flowing to the south. He turned his attention back to the cart. The expected explosion failed to materialize. Em-three-green had cut the power in time to keep anything from reaching dangerous overload and blowing itself to bits. Whether he had done so in time to keep the cart mobile was open to question.

Tchar glided down to a smooth landing next to them. The Skorr was panting heavily.

"I would like to know what the Vedala put in that cart, Captain. I could not fly fast enough to keep up with you."

"It was a standard Federation engine and drive system," Kirk told him. "The credit for its abnormal burst of speed goes to Mr. Spock and Em-three-green."

He glanced over at his first officer, who now stood unaided nearby. Spock said nothing, while Em looked embarrassed and tried to hide, the tips of his cilia running through a series of color changes.

"Close," Lara said into the awkward silence, staring toward the far river of lava.

"Far too close," agreed Spock. He was rubbing at the back of his head. "I prefer less substantial precipitation. And while I appreciate your actions on my behalf, Captain, your first duty should remain to the group and the mission."

"Quite right, Spock. I felt it paramount to maintain our expedition intact. Don't think anything as primitive as emotion entered into my decision." He made a movement over his chest. "Cross my heart and hope to die."

"The injection of humor," Spock began reprovingly, "does not obviate the fact that you risked the success of the mission to—"

"—save the best science officer in Starfleet," Kirk cut in.

A massive paw smote the sand between them. "Are you two going to argue each other's merits till I throw up, or do we get on with it."

Kirk grinned, turned to face the irritated reptile. "We—"

A blast of cold air hit them, staggered Kirk. Everyone looked back toward the volcanos. Neither peak could be seen. Both lay hidden somewhere behind and beneath the towering range of cumulo-nimbus clouds that had piled up out of nothing.

It seemed to be raining beneath the black cloudbank. "No, not raining," Kirk muttered to himself. Instead, the storm was putting forth a blizzard of considerable ferocity. A violent hissing sprang up from the land beneath the clouds—snow striking the lava. He shook his head, and wondered. A world most mad indeed! Mad was a mild adjective for this paranoid planet.

The dune, at least, would provide some slight protection. Everyone scrambled over to lie in the sheltering lee. The marching clouds caught them moments after.

"And I was just going to ask," Lara shivered, flapping her hands at her sides, "what next? Wish this place would make up its mind—a body can't find time to get comfortable here."

"We've no time to seek comfort," Kirk told her. "As Sord says, we've got to get on with it."

It took Em-three-green all of five minutes to determine that the cart wasn't going anywhere without several major repairs, for which they had been equipped with neither time, skill, nor parts. Kirk felt they could have managed the first two, but the matter of replacement components defeated him.

"Completely burned out," the tiny mechanic announced dolefully, his nose wrinkling at the pungent odor drifting up from the bowels of the engine housing.

Kirk sighed. "That means from here on we carry what we need."

No one voiced an objection, or an alternative. Kirk and Spock moved to the rear deck of the cart, opened the supply lockers, and began portioning out loads.

XI

Kirk eyed the deceiving circle of the sun above, put his head down and into the wind. It had changed direction four, maybe five times since they'd begun the trek.

He'd been right about the deceptiveness of this world—and that included distance. It felt as if they had been walking for years without drawing any nearer to their objective.

Thanks to the intermittent blizzard and freezing rain, many sandy areas had acquired a thin plating of ice. Walking on such terrain was next to impossible. They couldn't have managed it at all had not Sord volunteered an obvious solution. As a result, the big reptile was soon carrying the bulk of their equipment on his back. Doing so did not slow him up any.

Eventually the last snow and rain ceased, but the cold wind continued to blow.

"I don't understand," Kirk muttered, "we should have been there long ago."

"Perhaps, Captain," Spock replied, "the defenses surrounding the soul include image projectors. What we may have seen from afar might have been a false construct."

"What about Lara's certainty of direction, then, and Tchar, insisting he sensed it?"

"That is so. It may only be a matter of distance, then." He looked thoughtful. "If none of the preceding three expeditions had one of Lara's people, or a Skorr, with them, that might explain their demise. They could have hunted false projections in this malign wilderness forever."

Kirk paused, cupped his hands to his lips and yelled up into the chilled air.

"Tchar, see anything?"

A faint reply: "Wait . . ."

168

Tchar rose higher, stared into the distance. It was there, as he had known it would be—past tentacles and fields of ice-blocks at the bottom of the valley. A gigantic, featureless black monolith. He knew the soul of Alar lay within that ominous repository. They were on the course the humanoid Lara had indicated. He would have to tell the others.

"Yes!" He plunged downward, pulled up at the last second. "Ahead, Captain, it—" There was a low rumble, and he instinctively lifted off the ground. Kirk and Spock had no such ability and were knocked off their feet.

Somehow Lara kept her balance. Sord was not affected, of course.

"Another quake!" Lara cursed.

All around them was the horrible crunching sound of ice breaking up.

Someone screamed. All eyes turned toward Em-three-green. He had been trailing slightly behind. A vast ridge of ice had risen beneath him, cracked, twisted, opening crevices in the ice and in the earth below.

Using every cilium, Em-three-green tried to scramble clear. But the huge slab of ice was tilting sharply, and fine cilia are not equipped with claws or hooks. They found no purchase on the slick surface. Clawing frantically, he found himself sliding backward toward the abyss.

Everything happened fast, then. Spock took several long strides and threw himself stomach-first onto the ice near the tilting slab. He slid to the edge of the crevice, reached out, and grabbed Em-three-green by the scruff of the neck just as the latter was sliding in. Kirk got there barely in time to grab Spock's ankles to prevent him from going in with Em-three-green.

With a doomsday groan, the enormous frozen mass crashed into the depths.

Kirk grimaced with the strain of holding both Spock and Em-three-green. He tried to dig his toes into the frozen sand, found himself to his horror sliding slowly, slowly forward.

A coil of rope flew over his head. He reached up, slipped the noose over Spock's legs. Immediately the cord went taut. He pulled himself to the lip of the crevasse, stared down past the dangling form of Spock to where Em-three-green still hung in the Vulcan's grasp, swaying slightly and moaning. His eyes were shut tight.

Kirk felt Spock's body moving backward, crawled along with it. A glance showed Sord carefully bringing in the cord. Then Tchar had taken Em-three-green's weight from Spock and the first officer was easily pulled clear.

They took a long break there—not because they were especially tired, but because Em-three-green was too frightened now to move. Spock administered the medicine they had found in the supplies, but that would take time to work, too.

It it could have any effect at all. For when Em's violent shaking had calmed sufficiently for him to talk, it became clear that their mechanic was now beyond even terror. It was reflected in his tired voice, his miserable attitude.

"I can't go on any farther," he barely managed to whisper.

Kirk bit back his instinctive reply. A more woebegone being he had never seen. No surprise, really—Em-three-green had been frightened and uncertain on the Vedala asteroid, let alone here. He had probably been pushed through more today than any member of his race had been forced to endure in the past hundred years.

That he was still alive instead of dead from shock was proof enough he was a remarkable specimen of his type. Kirk eyed Em-three-green in a fresh light, took stock of their battered but still intact little company.

Sord sat invincible, a bored block of steel, ignoring the biting wind. Lara leaned against an ice-block, confident, athletic, secure in her knowledge of where she stood in relation to the universe, her lacquered exterior punctuated only by an occasional worried glance at Em-three-green.

Spock, nearby, was as calm as ever, ready for whatever might offer itself as an intriguing problem. And Tchar, free and safe as the air, hovered patiently above.

And himself, of course—concerned, anxious, but still
in firm command. He shook his head again. He hadn't
the slightest doubt that the finest representative of all
the races present was the miserable lump of shivering
cilia huddled in their middle and presently suffocating
in his own misery and self-pity.

"I'm not even afraid anymore," the subject of Kirk's
scrutiny murmured. "Just very, very tired. So very
tired."

"Come on, Em," Lara urged with surprising gentle-
ness. "We know where it is, and we've seen it. It's
just a little further."

"No!" Em-three-green shouted, with uncharacteristic
force, "I'm finished, I tell you! I've had enough. Let
the *murvlgeed* Skorr go on their *gurvlmeed* jihad! Let
the Galaxy blow itself to its assorted perditions, for all
I care. I'm . . . ," and the last word came out long and
slow and low, ". . . *tired*."

Kirk tried to find a way to say what had to be said
diplomatically, and came to a dead end. He firmed
himself.

"I'm sorry, Em-three-green, but there's still the possibility we'll be needing you." He glanced up significantly. "Sord . . ."

Em-three-green had enough srength left to protest as
he all but vanished in that massive paw. Sord placed
him carefully on his already heavily loaded back. The
picklock fought to his feet.

"Let me go, you outrageous hallucination!"

"Shut up and hang on," Sord muttered over his
shoulder. His head was bigger than Em-three-green's
entire body. "Dig down under the seal-tarp, between
those boxes. You can get out of the cold and wind." He
started off downslope at a steady trot.

"And be still! If you itch, I may forget the source
and scratch you!"

"I'll scout on ahead," Tchar suggested, rising into
the wind.

Kirk nodded absently as he, Spock and Lara fell in
at Sord's flank. Above them, from under the edge of
the tarp, a high voice muttered with an equal mixture

of pain and pathos, "Some day, you grotesque blob of creation, I'm going to cut you down to size."

Sord did not deign to reply.

Wind faded and clouds ran. The sun returned to melt the ice under their feet—fast enough, fortunately, to prevent the formation of much mud. As soon as the earth had dried sufficiently, they continued on.

They entered a region of low, sandy hills and encountered for the first time some local vegetation— scrub bushes and the toughest looking grasses Kirk had ever seen. They'd have to be to survive here, he mused. Even the brush grew parallel to the ground instead of up into the unpredictable sky.

"Wait," came a rumbling warning.

Kirk moved up alongside Sord.

"What is it."

"Quiet." Kirk looked in the direction Sord was looking, toward a thicket of bushes. For a moment, he thought he saw what had given the reptile pause— something dark and vaguely sinister moving among the branches.

"What is it?"

"You espy it too, then?"

"I thought I saw something move, though it might have been wind action. Hell, on this world it might have been anything."

"So. There is not supposed to be any animal life on this planet."

Reptile and man stared harder, but there were no more hints of movement.

"I wouldn't be surprised if the plants themselves had learned how to run away from things here," Kirk commented. Sord continued to stare, finally grunted.

"Guess you're right. This world just gets on your nerves."

When they topped the next rise, the black cube loomed just ahead. But there were no cheers, no shouts, no cries of *eureka!* Everyone was too bone tired, emotionally and physically. They were resigned rather than elated, for now their mission really began. Or would those sheer walls of unmarked, unbroken black prove deceptively easy to penetrate? None of them thought so, in the depths of their various minds.

"I can sense the soul," Tchar told them. He fluttered his wings as he stood near Kirk. "This is no illusion—it is here!" He beat the air, lifted.

"I will fly round, examine the structure, and return to meet you. There may be an entrance above the ground. If so, I will find it far more easily than any of you." He soared upward.

"Tchar!" Kirk yelled.

The Skorr stalled, hovered.

"Captain?"

"Watch it—we need you, too."

Tchar paused, added thoughtfully, "I will be careful, Captain." He dipped slightly, then rose and shot falconlike toward the roof.

"Tchar is right in his analysis," Spock finally declared, "but we should continue to search at ground level, if only to find shelter from the next meteorological aberration."

"Excellent idea, Spock," Kirk agreed, starting toward the nearest wall, "I'll see you shortly."

"A moment, Captain. I—" Kirk cut him off curtly.

"Not this time, Spock. If something unexpected gobbles me up, dissolves me, or otherwise renders me in corpus kaput, we're going to need you around to figure out how it was done and then to devise a way to circumvent it."

Spock appeared ready to protest further.

"And that's an order," Kirk finished.

He started down the slope. Before he had gotten ten meters from the others, he felt a warm presence alongside—Lara.

"I'll go with you." It wasn't a question.

"Uh-uh, as long as I'm in charge you'll—"

"Don't uh-uh me, Kirk. Remember, scouting's sort of my job. By rights, I ought to be doin' this by myself. You've already gotten all the use out of my sense of direction you're goin' to. I'm more expendable than anyone. But if you want to join me in gettin' yourself shot at, well, it'll be nice to have company."

Kirk started to yell—then found the incipient lecture

had turned into a mental smile that was mirrored on his face. They walked on together.

Spock, meanwhile, was trying to take his mind off the fact that Kirk was out ahead of them, out of range of immediate help, and nearing a structure they had every reason to believe contained hostile defenses ready for unannounced visitors.

"Sord, what did you think you saw back there?"

The massive brow frowned, forming a small facial crevasse. Its owner spoke without looking down.

"Don't know for sure, Vulcan. A shape—" Sord shook his head as if to clear it of a fog. Profound cogitation apparently wasn't one of his specialties. "Probably seeing things, as the captain figures."

Spock didn't look satisfied. "There should be *no* mobile life on this world." He started down determinedly after Kirk and Lara.

Em-three-green slipped off Sord's back, took two steps to every one of Spock's as he followed at his heels.

"You keep saying that, Spock."

"Yes," Spock admitted. "The key word is 'shouldn't.' The Vedala should have informed us."

Sord sighed, sounding like an ancient steam-engine, and followed too. "Maybe, the Vedala didn't know about whatever it was we saw."

"No, I still consider that an impossibility," Spock muttered.

"You think that," the dragon snorted. "Me, I ain't so sure. The longer I'm on this dump, the less I'm convinced of the omnipotence of our alien mentors. Now, mind you," he went on, "I'm just saying there are aspects of this they don't know nothing about.

"Leastwise, that's what I tell myself to explain why *I'm* here instead of them and their supposed superscience. I don't know what you tell *your*self, Vulcan."

Spock glanced up at the toothed jaws but was unable to read any expression there. However much the facts argued against the reptile's words, there were some odd points to consider about this entire undertaking.

Looking at it from a purely rational standpoint, now . . .

There was a last little sand dune. Kirk and Lara topped it. The fortress loomed over them, barely a hundred meters away. It was surrounded by a field of black gravel.

"That's it." He grinned at her. "End of one long hard journey I've no desire to repeat."

"Ah, but we still have to go back, James." She moved close and this time he didn't edge away. It was not because he was too tired to.

"I'll tell you something true," she began, staring into his eyes. "I find you one of the most attractive men I've ever met. If we were . . . ," she hesitated, "*together*, the rest of this would be easier. And if anything happened, why," she shrugged, "we'd have some green memories."

"I already have a lot of green memories," he told her gently. "I sometimes think too many."

Lara didn't try to hide her disappointment. "Oh." He put a comforting hand on her shoulder and squeezed.

"Maybe some other time, Lara. If it means anything, I think it would be one of the greenest of the green." He pulled his hand away as she reached for it. "But not now—we still have work to do."

She brightened. "At least you're willing to argue the point."

"I'm always open to logical persuasion."

The enormous, nearly perfect cube of metallic black was even more impressive when one stood at its immediate base. Nowhere could Kirk detect a hint of a sealed joint, bolt, or riveting of any sort. It was almost as if the monolith had been created in one piece, complete and perfect.

Nor was there any sign of an entrance. An awesome bit of engineering. It would have been dominating in a city. Here, on the bare sandy plain ringed by its black gravel border, it was awesome.

When nothing appeared to blast them from the earth, Kirk waved twice—behind and above. Sord, Spock, Em-three-green and Tchar joined him and Lara at the base.

"Is this not the shape," Spock asked the Skorr, "of the more primitive temples of your people?"

"Yes," Tchar admitted in surprise. "I had not known your knowledge extended so far, Mr. Spock." He stared upward. "Though there has never been anything as grand and beautiful as this. It is the work of some familiar with the Skorr, yet with an ability and single-mindedness of purpose my people have never known." He pointed to the right.

"If it is true to the old schematics, the entrance should be there." He flew toward the corner and they followed.

The carved door was cut just inside the corner, as Tchar had indicated. The complex motif engraved in the door itself probably meant something to the bird-man, but he didn't find it worthy of explanation and no one inquired.

"Truly, it is the same as the old temples," Tchar announced. "But the inscription is different. I cannot make it out, wholly. Much of it appears to consist of a warning, which is to be expected."

"Can you open it?" Kirk asked.

"No." Tchar looked distraught. "It is a familiar door—but it has no lock."

Kirk's gaze, followed soon by everyone else's, turned to rest on the shivering form of Em-three-green. He looked better now, though. Obviously the rest and shelter he had enjoyed while riding Sord had done him much good. Not that he felt any different about this craziness. He still wanted out at the first opportunity. But he was studying the door in spite of himself, professional curiosity being about the only thing capable of distracting him from his fright.

"There's a lock on my oculars," he declaimed firmly. "I recognize the type—rare, subtle and expensive."

Kirk stared hard at the door, tried to spot the mechanism Em-three-green was talking about and saw nothing but designs and inscriptions in an alien hand.

"I'll take your word for it—I have to," he admitted. "Can you open it?"

"There's no lock, seal, jam, portal, crawlway or door in the Galaxy I can't open," the picklock announced.

As Em-three-green unslung the small pack from his back, Kirk studied the overhanging brow of the doorway and wondered at the motivation behind it. There was a brooding, fanatical malevolence behind all this. A cunning madness that sought only the deaths of millions of innocent beings.

The key question now was—how much confidence did these extremists place in their hiding place? Was it sufficient in their eyes, or were there less passive forms of argument awaiting their entrance?

The pack produced a belt of flexible dark plastic equipped with a multitude of tiny compartments. Em-three-green laid it neatly on the ground, revealing a tool kit of gleaming, exquisitely handicrafted devices that would not have been out of place in a surgery.

The picklock's gaze studied a series of depressions which formed a regular, roughly diamond-shaped pattern in the approximate center of the door. Kirk wouldn't have recognized them in a million years as being apart from their neighboring carvings or as constituting a lock. Em-three-green selected a number of the tools with an assurance which Kirk found remarkably comforting. Having thus armed himself, he walked to the door and began work, his body shielding most of his actions from sight.

Kirk only hoped the alien's skill matched his confidence.

Something moved above them. He glanced upward sharply, saw nothing. *Easy, James, watch out or the boojums'll get you.* He returned his attention to Em-three-green.

Abruptly, an anticlimactic click sounded from somewhere inside the door. This initiated a steady hum.

Em-three-green's reaction was anything but relieved. Instead, his cilia moved more rapidly than ever. He seemed to be working twice as hard, and he looked frightened—which might not mean anything at all, since that was his normal mental state. But still—

"Anything the matter? Can't you do it?"

"I'm doing it, I'm doing it," the picklock muttered tightly, nervously.

"That's wonderful," Lara complimented him.

"No, you don't understand," he told her. "This lock is keyed with a timed series of irregular pulsations. If I don't cut the combination—eliminate the pulses in the proper sequence and within a certain time—it explodes."

Lara looked uncertain. "Does it matter whether we force the door neatly or otherwise?" She took a couple of wary steps backward, spoke to Kirk. "Why not let it blow itself open?"

Em-three-green supplied the answer—which pleased Kirk, because he didn't have one. "Such an explosion is designed to melt the metal of the door and any tunnel beyond, sealing it against unauthorized visitors—sometimes permanently."

"Spock, what's your opinion?" Kirk asked. Spock ignored him. The captain noticed his first officer was staring upward. "Spock?"

The science officer's warning shout sounded even as Kirk was turning his gaze toward the top of the cube.

Wings in wind—

Kirk ate sand as one of the cube sentinels swooped down at him, wicked hooked talons barely scraping his back. In unnatural silence the flying gargoyle banked and started in for another pass. There were two of the monsters—huge, threatening, not particularly swift, but immensely powerful-looking.

Kirk rolled to get his back against the cube, reaching for his phaser. Out of the corner of an eye he saw that Lara had her chemical gun out. She crouched just inside the entranceway. Em-three-green couldn't be seen, but his terrified moans could be heard from behind Sord. The big reptile had moved to block the entrance.

"Keep working," he rumbled over his shoulder. "I'll cover you."

Em-three-green was too busy working at the lock to offer a reply. In any case, he was in no position to argue with Sord. The big carnivore might possibly survive the threatened explosion, but Em-three-green would be reduced to scattered hunks of fur.

A shrill keening sounded directly above. Tchar charged into the two sentinels, breaking their formation and disrupting their attack. If one of the dark guardians got its claws on him, Kirk thought, the dogfight would be over instantly. But Tchar was clearly much faster. And he seemed to have the uncanny ability to dodge at the last second, before wing or claw could strike. It was almost as if he knew what his attacker was going to do before he did it.

The Skorr occupied the full attention of one of the sentinels. The other, the one that had just missed Kirk, was coming on again. Kirk fired. A second beam passed over his left shoulder—Spock was firing simultaneously.

Both beams made contact—and reflected off the polished throat of the gargoyle. It neither slowed nor swerved. A rapid series of explosions sounded from near the door. Lara was firing her out-dated but lethal-looking pistol.

Maybe the explosive pellets did more damage than the phasers, or perhaps the monster was distracted by the noise. Whatever the reason, it shifted course in mid-dive and angled for the exposed huntress.

Kirk bit his lip, forced himself to keep a steady stream of energy trained on the sentinel, which was taking both phaser beams broadside, now. Lara dropped to one knee, tried to hit its underside.

They couldn't tell whether it was the concentrated phaser fire, the explosive shells, or both, but suddenly the creature came apart in mid-flight. The explosion wasn't particularly impressive—but the amount of debris and the size of the area it was strewn over was. Also the composition of that debris.

Kirk kicked at a fragment of it, heard the slight ring as it went tumbling across the gravel.

"Mechanicals," Spock observed interestedly. "Sord felt he might have seen something watching us, back along our path. And you too, Captain." He looked satisfied. "The Vedala were right. There are no living creatures here—only mechanized protectors."

A cry from above reminded them the battle wasn't over. Tchar had gotten a grip on the back of the remaining sentinel. Unable to strike a significant blow at the irritation on its back, the mechanical wheeled and fluttered in frustration. But neither could Tchar effectively incapacitate the armored flier.

It shook free. Then, as though directed by outside authority, it suddenly changed its mind. Folding its wings, it dove toward the door. Sord tried to edge even tighter into the slight indentation of the doorway.

"Hurry, small one," he rumbled. Again Em-three-green had no time to answer.

Kirk and Spock shifted their phasers to cover the second mechanical—then hesitated as Tchar charged straight down in pursuit.

"Don't fire!" the Skorr screamed.

Moving incredibly fast, Tchar slammed across the skull of the monster. A low grinding noise came from it. Either the distraction was effective, or else the creature had decided it wasn't going to be able to get past Sord. It spread ponderous wings and soared skyward again.

Tchar closed with it once more near the top rim of the cube. They locked together and vanished over the edge. Eyes human and otherwise locked there for long moments.

Distantly, the cough of an explosion. They waited a long time. Tchar did not reappear.

"No way to tell what happened up there," Kirk murmured. "Can't even be sure the mechanical blew up." He ran a hand over the slick-smooth wall. "Tchar may be up there, wounded, unable to fly. We can't reach the roof from the outside—maybe there's a way up from the interior. We can damn well look for—"

A soprano cry of exhaustion and triumph came from his right. It was followed by a jerky, piping laugh. Sord backed away.

A deep protest of stone against metal sounded briefly, and then the door began to twist open, moving smoothly on unseen gears. They crowded around the entrance.

A driving, icy rain began to fall from a sky that had been clear and warm minutes before. Even so, the tunnel revealed was anything but inviting, dark as the pit and just as empty.

Kirk looked around at the rest of them, hunching his shoulders against the pelting rain. "We could rest here awhile."

"No," objected Lara firmly. "We've come this far without stopping. If I sit down and rest I don't think I'll feel much like getting up again."

"Let's finish it," Sord snorted, "or give this deadfall a chance to finish us." He grinned, displaying a wicked set of customized cutlery.

"I too, would prefer to press on, Captain," admitted Spock. "There may be other mechanicals on guard. We still have the advantage of some surprise, I think. The faster we move the more off-balance any enemy will be. He will be forced to improvise instead of prepare."

"All right, that's what I want, too. But this is nominally a democratic expedition," Kirk told them, matching Sord's grin in spirit if not in flash. Turning, he led the way into the cube.

Spock and Kirk both had belt lights, which they used to advantage. No automatic lights brightened their way, but neither were they challenged by cousins of the metal gargoyles.

After a short jog, they reached a spot where the tunnel opened into a vast open space. Spock turned his light on each of them in turn as Kirk took a brief roll call. No one had disappeared through a hidden door.

Man and Vulcan increased the intensity of their beams, playing them around the interior. They stood in one immense open space which the two lights could barely illuminate. The walls were a mirror of the outside. They had a slick look, possibly due to internal condensation, and were devoid of markings or features of any kind.

Which starkness made the discovery of the soul all the more dramatic.

Spock's beam flashed on something overhead. The science officer searched carefully with the light—and then he had it. A scintillating lacework of three golden möbius strips floating in free air. It was beautiful—but to the little knot of beings below, hardly awesome enough to inspire fanatical devotion in an entire race. The knowledge of that power, however, outshone any physical trappings and gave it impressiveness to spare.

"Pretty bauble," Sord ventured, breaking the silence, "but how do we reach it?"

By way of reply, Spock turned his light on the wall behind them, played the beam up, down and sideways on it. He ran his palm over the metal.

"Unusual alloy—it would take a warfleet to penetrate this. Using the door was preferable—the Vedalan way. There is not the slightest indentation, nothing that would permit climbing. A remarkable piece of engineering, executed with devotion and care."

"I'm sure the builders would be flattered," Kirk snapped drily. "How do we get up? The walls aren't climbable without special equipment, which we don't have." He ran a bootheel along the floor. The soft squeaking sound echoed dimly in the vastness.

"Either we find a way to reach it," and he nodded in the direction of the soul, agonizingly near yet infinitely out of touch, "or we've come all this way for nothing."

A vaguely familiar rumble then—the sound of the door twisting back into place. It closed with a dull boom.

At which a pale white light began to fill the chamber.

Em-three-green was the first one to the closed door. He had to hunt to find the barely perceptible hairline crack it formed with the wall.

"No lock on the inside," he observed professionally. "No evidence of pressure easement." He looked at them helplessly. "I can't open solid metal. We're prisoners."

"So we are," Kirk agreed. Spock turned to stare at the captain in confusion. His response wasn't quite what he expected.

"You don't seem very surprised, Captain." Kirk was walking back toward the now well-lit chamber, examining the walls thoughtfully.

"Three previous expeditions tried to recover the soul and were lost. Admittedly, this world is unrelentingly hostile—but any forewarned team prepared as we were should have been able to survive as we have." He surveyed the room.

"I see no bones or anything else. No sign of the previous expeditions. Their remains should be here if they got this far. That not one of them did so I find too hard to believe."

"You are suggesting, then, Captain . . . ?"

"I'm suggesting nothing, Spock—yet. Only that we've been luckier than we think, so far." He turned from Spock's inquiring stare to look back up at the soul.

"Still, we've no evidence anyone else *did* make it this far." He lowered his gaze and pointed. "Look there, on the far wall."

The ledge was barely a meter and a half wide and the same color and composition as the walls. It curled gently around the interior of the building, circling upward. It wasn't surprising the ledge had escaped Spock's probing beam. Without the interior illumination that had come on at the door's closing, they might never have spotted it.

They approached the ledge. It started two meters up. Kirk took a short run, leaped, grabbed the edge and started to muscle himself onto it.

A second later he fairly exploded upward. Getting his balance, he looked backward as Sord let out one of his now familiar rumbling laughs. Their reptilian strongman handed Spock up, then Lara and, despite frantic protests, Em-three-green.

"I'm terribly afraid of heights," the picklock sniffled, hugging the wall and shaking.

"You are terribly afraid of everything, Em-three-green," Spock commented. "There is no need to constantly apologize for your natural condition."

"I'm not apologizing!'" Em-three-green shot back defiantly; then he sank in on himself in embarrassment. "Please forgive me for yelling, but . . ."

"Later," Kirk instructed him. He stared across at their massive companion, but Sord stepped back, shaking his shovel-like head.

"No, I'm not built for that sort of thing." Kirk kicked at the metal ledge with one boot.

"I'll hold you, Sord. It's an extrusion of the wall itself."

But Sord replied reluctantly, "*Maybe* it'll hold me. No, you'd better go on without me. I'd crowd you and

I'd look funny walking on tiptoes. I'll wait for you
down here."

They climbed slowly and patiently. The ledge wasn't
dangerously narrow, but neither was it the broad boulevard Kirk wished for, and there was no railing.

It was remarkable, he reflected, how one could float
in a suit, free and weightless, outside the *Enterprise*
and feel perfectly calm and relaxed, and still grow
nauseated and dizzy on a climb like this.

He stared up and out at the object of their search.
The ledge reached out a thin tentacle of itself, but
stopped short of the soul. What they would do when
they reached that point he didn't know.

He felt himself shaking—and the cause was external.
"Hug the ledge!" Spock yelled. The four of them
dropped flat, trying to dig nails and toes into the
unyielding metal. The quake stopped, then came on
again stronger. But there was more bluster than threat
in the tremor. There was no sign of the walls coming
down or of the ledge collapsing beneath them.

"We already know this world is geologically perverse," Spock commented, rising to his feet. "It would
be illogical for this edifice to be built without keeping
that information in mind. Most likely it is mounted on
flexible supports which absorb most of the violence of
the quakes."

"That's what I need right now," muttered Em-three-
green.

Kirk was tempted to add that the picklock shook
even when the earth didn't. He quickly quashed the
thought, which was undiplomatic and unworthy of a
leader.

It was just that, as they drew nearer and nearer their
objective, his built-in warning system was winding
tighter and tighter. They couldn't simply reach out and
pluck it—they couldn't! Someone had gone to an incredible amount of trouble to build this supersafe on
this unholy world. To believe they could get this close
without additional opposition was naive in the extreme.

The ledge turned a sharp corner and narrowed considerably. Sord could never have negotiated it. They
had to turn sideways, backs against the wall, and edge

across carefully. Then it was up, up, mounting ever higher—until they reached a point where the ledge broadened to a stop, from which a long, narrow arch extended out toward the floating soul.

They needed a respectable hunk of nerve to walk out onto that thin projection, and even more to look down the dizzying drop to the floor below. Em-three-green huddled close to Lara and concentrated his full attention on remaining in the precise center of the platform.

The metallic protrusion ended a couple of meters from the soul. "Close," Em-three-green groaned, "so close!"

Lara was unwinding a length of cord from her belt. "Maybe I can get a line on it."

Spock restrained her.

"We have no idea what kind of force field may surround it. Best to wait and save direct contact as a final option."

They hardly had time to discuss other possible means of retrieving the soul when a violent *crump* sounded behind them. Everyone ducked instinctively, but the blast was not repeated.

Kirk looked back the way they had come and saw that a wide section of ledge had vanished. Smoke still rose from the edges of seared metal. They were marooned on the platform.

That it had taken this long for their tormentor to show himself was all that surprised Kirk. But the motives of the mad are obscure and difficult to analyze. Kirk stared up into the far reaches of the fortress. They were two-thirds of the way up—from where he saw that near the roof the walls were not entirely unmarred. Instead, they were pocked with carved images, crevices, small craters and tiny dark tunnels.

"I told you there had to be something watching, protecting here besides just a locked door. There had to be something besides reliance on freakish weather and the occasional earthquake. There had to be something besides this superegomaniacal metal box. Something more subtle, something even the Vedala couldn't defend against."

"Which would be what, Captain?" Spock inquired.

Kirk's reply was tinged with sarcasm.

"A worm in the apple, Mr. Spock. A monkeywrench in the works, an activated positron in the dilithium, a rottenness in Denmark." He shook a challenging fist at the vast expanse of the roof.

"I know who you are!" he shouted, his eyes searching, hunting. Who could have placed the soul in a restraining field here, three hundred meters up in open air? Who would think to build this travesty of a holy temple as a monument to annihilation? Who, but the Skorr themselves?

"Show yourself, Tchar! The masquerade is over—take your bow."

Nothing happened for several seconds. Then the prince of the Skorr dropped from an as yet undetected hiding place. He dove toward them and spread batlike wings at the last moment, braking to hover on the other side of the soul. Laughing, whistling, jabbing accusing fingers at them—mocking civilization, and worse.

"Tchar," Lara muttered wonderingly, "in the name of the seven gods of the hunt, why did you do this? You and your little clique of militarists?"

Kirk shook his head sadly, tiredly. "It seems history is doomed to repeat itself even across racial and spatial borders. It's not a little fascinating, and not a little sad. You and your accomplices would start a meaningless crusade of blood across the Galaxy, initiate the murder of your people and other innocents—for what, for what? Tell us why, Tchar."

"The Skorr were a warrior race!" Tchar shrilled, whirling about in anger. "Slaves to the illusion of peace are we now—cowards, grown soft through the comforts of trade and weak by mental miscegenation." He gestured at the soul.

"This sick dream," he spat, "stole our souls, it did not heal them!" Now a hint of the fanatic's pride crept into his voice. "But there were a few of us high ones, a very few, who were wise enough to perceive this gigantic illusion which had sapped our racial determination and courage.

"We planned the theft, and none stopped us. None will stop us! There will be no time for another expedition before fury returns my people to glorious tradition. I, myself, came along to insure this. I alone saw the need, when I was told who would participate. And I was right—I was needed.

"I, Tchar, hereditary prince, waster of mine enemies, drinker of blood—I will lead my people into glory and revenge!"

"At best you can win only a Pyrrhic victory," Spock replied calmly, not in the least impressed by the *sturm-und-drang* speech of Tchar. "Most, if not all of your warriors will eventually be tracked down and killed. The Skorr homeworlds will be scoured clean of life when the warrior races of the Federation rise to do battle with you—as will the empires of the Klingons, and Romulans, and all the others."

"Perhaps," Tchar admitted, in defiance of Spock's logic. "A noble death risked to win a great dream." He shook angry talons at them.

"But no longer will we live like worms, crawling in the dirt. We will rise and conquer. You will be the fourth group sacrificed to the cause. But you have my respect—only you came this far. Only you necessitated my personal intervention. You will die in grace, as befits the enemies of a hereditary prince."

"Tchar, wait!" Lara called, too late. The Skorr had already wheeled up to disappear back into the dark places of the ceiling.

Far, far below a massive figure watched and tried to understand. Sord could tell something had gone wrong, but the sound from above dissipated in the vast expanse of the chamber. He had seen the ledge cut, of course, but there was nothing to be seen from below that could tie Tchar to the sabotage. Massive thoughts were considered and discarded as he tried to make sense of what had happened.

Lara had walked to the very edge of the precipice and stared calmly over. "Absolutely unclimbable, as Mr. Spock said. She shook her head disparagingly. "We'd bounce awful high."

As if to confirm her words, she suddenly drifted upward, followed by the others. Em-three-green spun frantically, clawing for a foothold.

"I believe this renders the problem academic," Spock declared.

"Gravity neutralizer—the building's equipped with null gravity," Kirk explained tightly.

"It may be part of the edifice's own components," Spock added, spreading arms and legs and trying to keep relatively motionless. "It would surely explain how this structure has been able to survive the multitude of tremors and other natural disasters that must have struck this spot."

Kirk found himself spinning despite his best efforts. Below, Sord found himself drifting, too, but had reacted more rapidly than any of them. He'd kicked out at the last instant, struck the floor a titanic blow, and sent himself sailing upward. His aim had been excellent. Reaching out, he had gotten a solid grip on the projecting ledge, pulled himself atop it, and was now the only one not floating free.

Somewhere nearby, Tchar was whistling amusedly at them. Kirk struggled to orient himself, finally located the teasing, darting birdman.

"Now you can fly and fight as a Skorr—a worthy way to die, is it not?"

Kirk started to reply, but was interrupted by Sord. "No offense, little one, but let me have him." He slapped his chest with one paw, a blow that would have buckled the wall of a starship. But there was more to this situation than bulk and strength. Tchar would cut the clumsy Sord to pieces before the reptile could get a grip on him.

"No, Sord, not in free fall."

"Use your phaser on him, quickly!" Em-three-green suggested nervously.

"Yes, Captain Kirk," the voice of Tchar mocked, "use your phaser on me."

An invitation to destruction, Kirk knew. Tchar wanted them to fight him as a Skorr, so he could reassert his madman's version of Skorrian bushido. That meant hand-to-hand combat. No modern accouterments like hand phasers.

If this structure was equipped with electronics as sophisticated as a gravity neutralizer, he had no doubt there was something trained on them this very minute capable of canceling out their phasers—perhaps even keying on their energy cells. To fire one might cause it to blow up in one's face.

"It must be on his terms," he told Em-three-green.

They might work this to their advantage. If they expressed a reluctance to fight, Tchar could probably dispose of them from a convenient distance. Instead he chose personal combat. His controlling phobia demanded he kill them personally.

"Spock, how long since you've done zero-gee combat exercises?"

"I subscribe to the prescribed dosage, Captain."

That told him Spock was up on technique, without telling Tchar any more than was necessary. Let him interpret that as he might.

"Well," he shouted to Tchar, steeling himself, "what are you waiting for?"

Tchar was hard put to restrain his laughter. "You are turning slow circles, Captain Kirk, with no sign of stopping. A most disadvantageous tactical position."

Tchar was right. Before they could do any maneuvering of any kind they needed a firmer purchase than thin air. Tchar didn't want the kill to be too easy, then. Worse for him.

"Lara, throw your line to Sord." The huntress nodded. Uncoiling the line and wrapping one end around her right wrist, she tossed the gently weighted other end towards the braced and ready Sord.

The action sent her spinning, but Sord caught the loop easily and pulled her in. While he braced her she reeled in Em-three-green, Kirk, and Spock.

"Very good, Captain, very good!" Tchar applauded mockingly. Kirk thought he detected the gleam of insanity in the Skorr's eyes even at this distance. He was working himself up good and proper.

So much the better. "If we can get him to lose control of himself, Spock, get him to stop thinking . . ."

"An admirable objective, Captain," Spock whispered back. "Should I have a choice, however, I believe I would opt for a fast kick to the jugular."

Kirk smiled grimly.

"Let's go, then."

Bracing himself, Kirk drew an imaginary line and kicked free of the platform. Spock did likewise, kicking harder. Thus he reached the far wall first and pushed off again to approach Tchar from the other side.

Tchar whistled, charged straight at Kirk. Obviously he intended to deal with them one at a time. He had plenty of time to bleed Kirk, turn, and deal with Spock.

Kirk had aimed for the soul. It was the only cover of any kind available in the dangerously open space. The maneuver generated only contempt in Skorr's eyes. He'd expected better than a desperate dash for the soul.

Talons extended, he headed for Kirk's face. The human's soft hands worried him not at all. Kirk first, then the Vulcan, then the others at his leisure. The large stupid reptile would take many cuts to die. Em-three-green he would save for last. It would be interesting to see if he could frighten him to death.

But first—the human.

Wings beating to his sides, forelimbs extended—then Kirk moved. Tchar momentarily lost his poise and tried to change his angle of approach.

At the last possible second, Kirk had curled into a tight spinning ball. When he came out of it it was with both legs tucked tight into his chest. He extended them just in time to meet Tchar's midsection.

One claw struck home—only to glance harmlessly off the thick sole of Kirk's boot. But the unblocked leg drove deeply into the Skorr's stomach.

As he tumbled awkwardly from the blow, screaming in pain and rage, the hereditary prince of the Skorr was met from behind by the late arriving Spock. Too late, Tchar sensed he had been duped, that the timing of the two bipeds had been planned to bring about just this situation.

He'd committed a terrible error—underestimating his opponents. Now the Vulcan had a grip on both arms and despite his best efforts, Tchar couldn't dislodge him from his back.

Kirk had continued on to the soul, met the expected force-field and used it to kick back toward Tchar. But this time Tchar was ready for the tumble-and-kick and he twisted away, slashing out with a clawed leg.

Kirk wrenched aside and the claw ripped down his front, drawing a little blood. Straining, the Skorr managed to fight his way over to the force field. A couple of rough jolts against it were enough to knock Spock loose. Furious, Tchar turned to rend the Vulcan.

But Spock was far from incapacitated. Although he had been shaken off, he had managed to get a grip on the outline of the force field. Now he used it as a barrier between himself and Tchar.

By then Kirk had struck the far wall, kicked off, and was coming back for more. Tchar spotted him at the last instant, but by now he had had about enough: this exercise had been interesting and instructive, but it had taken rather too much time. Instead of turning to meet Kirk's charge he strove for altitude.

"Very good," he called down to the two men bobbing near the soul. "Surprisingly good. But it was you, Captain Kirk, who called for an end to masquerades. Now this too, must end.

Folding his wings, he dropped like a stone toward Kirk. Sord, Em-three-green and Lara watched, worried. Kirk was drifting free. Even if he reached the force-field around the soul, Tchar's power dive would drive curved talons right through him.

Kirk reached the soul, got a grip on its edge. Tchar screamed in triumph—just as Kirk turned. Both sets of claws slammed into Kirk's backpack—and stuck.

The force of the blow had almost knocked Kirk off the field—almost. Then, as Tchar screamed in frustration, Spock crawled carefully round and got a grip on the Skorr's wings.

They made contact with the soul and contact with the thief. Now was the time.

"Lara, call for retrieval!"

"No!" Tchar shrieked desperately. Kirk had succeeded in his aim, making the Skorr forget everything but the fury of battle. They had to have him pinned before they issued that irreversible call. Had to, because there was a button on Tchar's belt, a button he now fought vainly to reach, a button which undoubtedly controlled the gravity neutralizer and in an emergency could have sent them all tumbling to the metal floor where, as Lara had predicted, they would have bouncd very high indeed.

But Lara could now throw the switch on her pack without fear of that.

A faint smell of ozone was in evidence as the air around them crackled. They had only one remaining fear—could the Vedala retrieval field penetrate the force-field holding the soul of Alar? Or would it retrieve only them?

Or would the force-field interfere with the retrieval field and leave them all drifting in limbo?

He speculated on it as his vision began to fade, as Tchar's wrenching cry of, "Let me die!" echoed in his ears.

No Tchar, Tchar of the soaring wings and mad dream, you're coming back with us—though I truly wish that I could grant your wish . . .

Running water played counterpoint to the wind in the grass. Kirk felt a warm breeze on his face and smelled the smell of green things growing. He looked down at himself.

There were no scratches on his arm, no gash in his chest where Tchar's claws had struck. They were standing in a familiar glade, back on the Vedala asteroid.

Baring unabashed stares of astonishment, they stood as they had stood days ago—rested, clean, refreshed—before the expedition had begun. Had he dreamed it all—had the quest only taken place in their minds? Or, he thought as he turned to face the small, confident figure standing in the glade's center, had it all been simply an elaborate display of some strangely Vedalan sense of humor?

"We give you thanks," the Vedala intoned solemnly. He moved aside to reveal a triplet of möbius strips, glowing golden against the greensward. "The soul of Alar is returned to his people. There will be no jihad."

He gestured and the soul vanished. Presumably it was already well on its way to the central Skorr homeworld—along with a recommended list of precautions to prevent any future theft.

"What about Tchar?" Kirk asked. "How are you going to deal with him?"

Another gesture and they saw Tchar, arms and wings bound, sneering at unseen tormentors.

"The hereditary prince is proud and brave and has many useful qualities. We will make a small adjustment in his personality. You would argue the morality of this, Captain Kirk, as is the peculiarity of your race—but you will not argue its efficacy. He will be made sane again." The picture of the bound Tchar faded.

"We cannot reward you with other than our thanks and the knowledge of what you have prevented. Nor can the Skorr, for this must remain hidden from them. Tchar's co-perpetrators will be found out and dealt with, without subjecting their people to racial shock. The Skorr must never suspect that this monstrousness was engineered by some of their own, or they would engage in a vicious, useless witch-hunt for more blasphemers."

"Oh well," Sord rumbled airily, "got nowhere to wear a medal anyway."

"There will be questions," Spock remarked.

The Vedala smiled softly at the Vulcan. "You will see, there will be no questions. Goodbye . . ." The Vedala began to dissolve.

Lara moved over to stand next to Kirk. "Goodbye, James. It's too bad—we almost could have . . ."

Her voice faded and became inaudible as Kirk's vision began to blur once more.

Scott and Sulu were in the transporter room when Spock and Kirk rematerialized. And although Kirk was glad to see them, he noticed something about their expressions.

"Captain, Mr. Spock," Sulu began anxiously, "what went wrong?"

Kirk took a moment to look down at himself, saw nothing wrong, glanced over at Spock. Everything seemed perfectly normal here—except Sulu and Scott's attitude.

"What do you mean, Mr. Sulu?"

"You went over and came right back," Scott explained. "Did the Vedala call this off, give you orders, or what?"

"Now wait a minute, what—"

Spock made a gesture indicating silence.

"How long have we been gone, Mr. Sulu?" Spock inquired.

Sulu shrugged. "About two minutes, maybe three, I guess. Just enough time for me to get down here after you beamed dirtwards."

A great deal passed between Kirk and Spock in a single look.

"The Vedala changed their minds," the captain said briskly, stepping off the transporter platform. "They needed some fast advice and we answered their one question. Back to your stations, now. This was just a momentary detour, a sidestop. Mr. Spock . . ."

"Yes, Captain?"

"I'm going to my cabin to make the official log entry. I'll see you on the Bridge."

"Very good, Captain." Spock started for the elevator.

"Oh, and Spock . . ."

"Sir?" Spock turned and waited.

"When you get there, instruct Uhura to contact the nearest Starfleet base for orders. Maybe this time they can find something a little more interesting for us to do."

"*Interesting,* Captain?" Spock threw back his head in surprise as Kirk walked up beside him. "It *is* interesting . . . to learn that understatement is not the exclusive province of Vulcans."

The doors closed behind them.

Scott leaned against the transporter console while Sulu stared in confusion after the two departed commanding officers.

"Now what do you suppose all that was about?" the helmsman wondered out loud. Scott smiled.

"It's verra simple, Mr. Sulu. Easy to understand when you've been around the captain and Mr. Spock as long as I have. See, they're both crazy. Only the captain tries to fool us into thinkin' it's a cover, and Mr. Spock is too polite to admit to it." Scott let out a long breath, moved away from the console.

"Well, you heard the orders. I suggest you get back to the Bridge. Me, I'm goin' back to Engineerin' and my engines. At least they're not loonie. It's easy to stay sane back there," he finished as he stepped into the elevator. "Because when anythin' goes wrong with them, I can always call on the little people to come and fix 'em."

The lift doors closed.

Sulu stared at them for a long moment, then muttered something no one was there to hear. It didn't matter—mankind had heard it before, had known it to be true since the beginning of time.

"Everyone's crazy here but me and thee," he sang, "and sometimes I'm not so sure about thee."

Whistling cheerfully, he ambled toward the elevator and the bridge beyond.

SUPERB S-F
from
⑬
BALLANTINE BOOKS